The Hangrope Posse

When Sherwood Drake was accused of stealing the railroad payroll, The Hangrope Posse lynched him before anyone could prove his guilt – but the money remained missing.

Seven years later, his sons Braxton and Martin ride into Shady Grove looking for answers. They doubt they will find the missing money, or their father's killers, but when the lynch mob unexpectedly returns to Shady Grove, the Drake boys face a force of mindless terror.

As more bodies swing and the boundaries of justice become blurred, Braxton and Martin Drake venture to find an answer to the important question: was their father's death justified, or just another unlucky hand in a cruel game of fate?

By the same author

Ambush in Dust Creek
Silver Gulch Feud
Blood Gold
Golden Sundown
Clearwater Justice
Hellfire
Escape from Fort Benton
Return to Black Rock
The Man They Couldn't Hang
Last Stage to Lonesome
McGuire, Manhunter
Raiders of the Mission San Juan
Coltaine's Revenge
Stand-Off at Copper Town
Siege at Hope Wells
The Sons of Casey O'Donnell
Ride the Savage River
High Noon in Snake Ridge
The Honour of the Badge

The Hangrope Posse

Scott Connor

ROBERT HALE · LONDON

First published in Great Britain 2014

ISBN 978-0-7198-1306-1

Robert Hale Limited
Clerkenwell House
Clerkenwell Green
London EC1R 0HT

www.halebooks.com

Typeset by
Derek Doyle & Associates, Shaw Heath
Printed and bound in Great Britain by
CPI Antony Rowe, Chippenham and Eastbourne

PROLOGUE

'Don't look away,' Patrick Hopeman said. 'I owe the poor wretches here today that much.'

'We owe Sherwood Drake nothing,' the nearest man said. 'He stole the railroad payroll, so the hangrope posse gave him what he deserved.'

The other four men grunted in support, but Patrick shook his head.

'I didn't just mean the dead men.'

When several men nodded, acknowledging that they would have to live with the consequences of their actions, Patrick considered the grisly scene.

For the last month he had led a band of railroad workers in tracking down Sherwood Drake's troublesome group. When he had cornered Sherwood outside Shady Grove he'd dispensed justice immediately.

Now four men dangled from the two strongest branches of the gaunt oak. The first two to be hanged had stilled, while the other two still twitched.

'So now we can build a railroad again,' another man said after a while. 'Until the hangrope posse are needed again.'

'I hope we won't be.'

'Either way, we should never talk about this with nobody.'

'We won't, but this day will change us, let us hope for the better.'

Bearing in mind the kind of men he'd recruited, Patrick doubted that, and when he looked at the line of riders none of them met his eye.

He turned away and rode back to the tracks while the wind whipped up, making the branches creak. When Patrick reached the tracks his men were chatting amiably, but he reckoned he could still hear the creaking.

CHAPTER 1

'If I ever join another drive, shoot me,' Martin Drake said.

His brother Braxton laughed. Martin had uttered this lament many times recently, but this time he sounded as if he meant it. When Braxton thought about it he agreed with him.

He felt like he'd been in the saddle for two years, not the two months it had taken them to reach Shady Grove. Even after he had been paid, he had been too weary to join the others in their frantic dash to the nearest saloon to spend their wages.

Instead, he and Martin had ridden around the outskirts of town, seeing what opportunities might present themselves for alternative employment. So far there had been nothing, but nothing still felt like a better option than another cattle drive.

'Plenty of people live here now so we might find work,' Braxton said.

'We might, but I reckon we should move on to

Eureka Forks, or perhaps even Destiny.'

Martin gave Braxton a long look, making Braxton frown. Until a few days ago he had only rarely thought about their errant father Sherwood's demise here seven years ago, but when the drive had closed on Shady Grove, both men had become increasingly nervous.

'On the other hand, staying in Shady Grove for a while might kill off the demons we both have about this place.'

'Perhaps you're right,' Martin murmured, his tone distracted. He pointed at a tangle of trees 200 yards beyond the edge of town between the station and the depot. 'What do you make of that?'

Braxton considered the stark oaks and when he saw what had intrigued Martin his heart thudded with trepidation.

'I hope it's nothing,' he said. He shivered despite the baking heat of the summer afternoon. 'But we should check it out. Then we should get some liquor inside us.'

Martin nodded. At a slow trot, they moved away from town with their necks craned and their postures stiff.

Something was dangling from a branch. It was over five feet long, about eight feet off the ground and it was swaying in the breeze. Sadly, the closer they got to the tree, the more obvious it became that it was a person.

Braxton continued to hope he'd been mistaken

and that the object was something else, perhaps clothes stuffed with straw, but that small hope fled when they took a wide berth around the tree. They were confronted with the hanging body of a young man, his face suffused and his mouth open.

'You keep lookout,' Martin said with a gulp. 'I'll cut him down.'

This was the first order Braxton had been given for months that he didn't mind following, so he moved away from the tree and looked towards town. He could see nobody and so he looked further afield, but whoever had done this had fled.

He finished his survey facing the tree where Martin was sawing through the rope. The body dropped and folded over on the ground, its fluid motion suggesting this had happened recently. Braxton bit back his reluctance and jumped down from his horse to check that the man was dead.

The noose had bitten into the man's neck and Braxton had to shake the rope while pushing the body's shoulder to prise it free. By the time the rope had come loose the body was lying on its side. He shoved it over on to its back to consider it.

A wheezing gasp of air slipped between the man's lips, making Braxton jerk back in surprise.

'You hear that?' he said, looking up at Martin.

'Sure did,' Martin said. He tipped back his hat before he got over his shock and dismounted. 'But he's in a bad way, so we have to be quick.'

Braxton nodded, then with no further delay he

grabbed the man's legs while Martin took his shoulders. They bundled him over the back of Martin's horse leaving him to lie with his arms dangling.

Then, without taking the time to concern themselves with the man's dignity or his well-being in being handled roughly, they hurried towards town. Martin rode with one hand pressed down on the man's back to ensure he didn't jostle free, while Braxton galloped on ahead.

By the time Braxton reached the main drag he was a hundred yards ahead of Martin. As he didn't know the town he called out to every passer-by. He was directed to the surgery which, thankfully, was on the station side of town. On reaching it he leapt down from his steed and hurried inside while calling out for help.

When Martin arrived Braxton was standing outside the surgery with the white-haired Doctor Jeffries, who clutched a black bag to his chest while a crowd of onlookers gravitated towards them with a mixture of concern and curiosity etched into their faces. Braxton and Martin joined forces to haul the man unceremoniously off the back of the horse, after which he slumped to the ground, seemingly lifeless.

Jeffries knelt beside the man. After a few seconds he confirmed that the man was indeed dead.

'I'm sorry,' he said, shaking his head. 'Eddie's been dead for a while.'

'But we heard him breathe before we brought him to you,' Braxton said, while Martin grunted his support.

'Bodies do strange things sometimes and . . .' Jeffries trailed off when he moved the body's collar aside and revealed the livid rope burn. He sighed. 'Not another one.'

Jeffries shook his head sadly, but he relaxed when Marshal McSween came briskly towards them. An onlooker spoke to McSween, which made him close his eyes for a moment before he moved on to consider the body. He shook his head.

'Who found Eddie?' he asked. Jeffries pointed at Braxton and Martin.

McSween nodded to them then removed his jacket and draped it over the body's face. That done, he drew them aside to hear their story, which Braxton related in a suitably sombre tone.

'We're just sorry we were too late,' Braxton said, finishing off the tale.

McSween glanced at the watching people; his narrowed eyes implied he didn't know who was involved, so he no longer trusted anyone.

'And I'm sorry people have got a taste for delivering summary justice. This is the second lynching in as many weeks.' McSween stood back to appraise them while rubbing his jaw. 'So why are you in town?'

'We arrived with the cattle drive. We were riding around looking for work when we came across Eddie.'

'Any luck?'

'Not yet.'

McSween jutted his jaw. 'With this recent trouble,

I need to appoint a couple of attentive deputy lawmen.'

Braxton raised an eyebrow with interest and looked at Martin, who shrugged.

'I hadn't thought of doing that,' Martin said. His declaration made Braxton frown, so he continued: 'Is this a temporary appointment?'

'It'll be permanent, although if you accept I hope you'll last for longer than the previous deputy did.'

'Why, what happened to him?'

McSween pointed at the body, which was now being measured up by an undertaker.

'You just brought him into town,' he said.

'I don't want to be a deputy town marshal,' Martin said when he and Braxton were standing at the bar of the Sagebrush saloon.

McSween had given them a day to consider their decision. After a sombre night, in which the death of the deputy had stirred up so many depressing memories that Martin had struggled to get to sleep, they had met the marshal again the next day.

'So I'd gathered,' Braxton said in reply to his brother's statement. He swirled his whiskey glass before taking a gulp. 'But I reckon I'll take McSween's offer.'

'I asked you to shoot me if I joined another drive,' Martin said, smiling. 'With that job, you'll be the one getting shot at.'

Braxton laughed. 'McSween says my first task will

be to find out who killed Deputy Eddie Crabbe. After what we saw I'd like to do that.'

Martin nodded. 'Finding that young man hanging there was sickening.'

Braxton studied his drink before he downed it, his pensive expression showing he was wondering whether they should discuss the matter that had clearly been on his mind since they'd found Eddie.

'Everyone said our father was a no-account waste of skin,' he said after a while. 'Perhaps he was, but nobody ever found the missing payroll he was supposed to have stolen, so I'd like to find out the truth. There was barely a town here when he was lynched, but if someone is dispensing unofficial justice again, a deputy lawman might find some answers.'

Martin shrugged. 'I'm not sure I want to hear those answers. Nothing you might uncover will change what happened and neither will it make it any easier to accept, but I wish you luck. Neither Eddie nor our father deserved that fate.'

Despite this last comment, trying to maintain justice in a town that thought the rope resolved everything didn't sound like something he wanted to do. So he eased his conscience by buying Braxton another drink.

'What will you do instead?' Braxton asked when they had full glasses before them.

'I'll find something,' replied Martin. He leaned towards Braxton. 'Although if I look as if I'm about to join another drive you know what to do.'

Braxton nodded, but in deference to the position he would soon adopt, he only sipped his drink, then pushed it away with the glass half-full.

'I'd better see the marshal and tell him my decision,' he said.

He dallied, clearly giving Martin a chance to change his mind. But Martin wished him well and gave him a hearty backslap.

When Braxton left Martin stood hunched over the bar to consider what he would do instead. Two drinks later he was no nearer to an answer. Then he heard his name being spoken.

He turned. Seeing that Doctor Jeffries was looking at him he beckoned to him. His interest grew when he observed that a young, fair-haired woman was with the doctor, although when he noticed her tear-brimmed eyes and her black clothing he got an inkling of why he'd been sought out. He removed his hat.

'This is Honoria, Eddie's wife,' Jeffries said. 'She's just arrived in town from Carpenter's Gulch, and sadly she arrived at the worst possible time.'

Martin tried to meet Honoria's eyes, but she cast her gaze down.

'I'm sorry about what happened to your husband,' Martin said. He shrugged as he searched for something comforting to say. 'He looked like a decent man.'

She said nothing and they stood in awkward silence until Jeffries took her elbow and directed her to a bar stool.

'I only recommend this for medicinal purposes,' he said with a kindly gleam in his eye, 'but a sip of liquor might help us all at this difficult time.'

Martin busied himself with collecting glasses and pouring out a large and a small measure. Honoria considered her glass dubiously.

'I don't drink liquor,' she said, her voice small.

'Neither do I,' Jeffries declared, although his red-veined cheeks and bulbous nose belied his words. 'But I'd never recommend anything for my patients that I'm not prepared to try myself.'

He directed a slow wink at Martin, which Honoria couldn't help but see, and knocked back a large gulp of his drink.

'I'm not your patient,' she said, and tipped the contents of her glass into Jeffries' glass.

The doctor drank her share without comment, after which they remained seated in awkward silence until he brightened and looked at Martin.

'Honoria wanted to speak with you privately, so I'll leave you two now.' He placed a hand on her shoulder and squeezed. 'You know where I am, if you need to see me again.'

'I very much doubt I will,' Honoria said.

She stepped away from his hand, and with a bemused glance at Martin Jeffries left them.

'What do you want to ask me about?' Martin said.

She poked her empty glass around in a circle as she collected her thoughts.

'I gather Marshal McSween offered you a position as his deputy, but you refused.'

'I did. I don't want to be a deputy lawman. Not that I have any other work. And not that the work would be beyond me. And not that your husband wasn't right to want to be McSween's deputy. . . .' He frowned and ended lamely. 'I just want to do something else.'

He knew he'd babbled, but his answer didn't appear to concern her as she absent-mindedly toyed with the glass.

'In that case, would you be prepared to work for me instead?'

She turned to him and brushed a ringlet of blond hair away from her eyes before she opened them wide, beseeching him to accept her offer. Her eyes were a deep blue and the sight made his heart hammer and his mouth go dry.

'Sure,' he managed to croak.

CHAPTER 2

'You lucky, lucky, lucky varmint,' Braxton said, his eyes as wide as Honoria's had been. Although they couldn't entrance Martin in the way hers had while she'd outlined her offer.

'If I don't accept, shoot me,' Martin said, failing to stop a huge grin breaking out.

'I doubt you'd notice.' Braxton sighed and sat down at his new desk. 'So what work has this pretty young widow woman offered you?'

'I have to escort her to Eureka Forks.' Martin gestured through the law office window, indicating the waiting stage. 'And I get paid!'

Braxton narrowed his eyes. 'Why is she leaving so soon after getting here and with her husband still unburied?'

Martin smiled. 'I can see you're starting to think like a lawman, but it's simply that she's worried that whoever killed Eddie will come after her next. So she wants to leave town quickly.'

'His death is the second recent hanging here, so I guess she has a right to be scared. But either way, I need to talk to her.'

'The stage leaves in an hour and she doesn't want to talk to anyone.' Martin shrugged as Braxton eyed him dubiously. 'She only arrived in town this morning and clearly she doesn't know anything that'll help your investigation, but if she tells me anything, when I return I'll let you know.'

Braxton nodded. Then, since time was pressing, Martin bade his brother goodbye and hurried out of the law office. Honoria had given him thirty minutes to complete his affairs before he had to collect her from the Sagebrush Hotel, where she had booked a room in which to freshen up.

The trip to the law office had taken only ten minutes, but he still hurried to the hotel to show her he took his duties seriously. His firm knock on her door received a nervous reply that Martin could barely hear.

'Who's there?' she asked.

'It's me, Martin. I'll wait out here until you're ready to leave.'

She didn't reply immediately, so Martin stood to the side of the door.

'No,' she said, her voice again barely audible. 'Come in and sit with me, please.'

He went in and found her sitting beside the window in a position from where she could watch the waiting stage while remaining unseen from the road.

'Have you seen something that's troubled you?' he asked.

'No, but my father was the railroad man Patrick Hopeman. He had enemies, and clearly Eddie had enemies too.' She pointed at the main drag, picking out several men. 'Someone out there killed him and I wouldn't want to meet him.'

'My brother Braxton is McSween's new deputy,' Martin told her. 'He's a good man, full of enthusiasm and good ideas. He'll find the people responsible.'

'I hope so. I won't want to return until he has.'

Martin frowned, struggling to find the right thing to say.

'You'll need to return to visit Eddie's grave.'

She turned to him, her troubled eyes suggesting that this wasn't a sensible comment to have made.

'His final resting place isn't important. Eddie was so full of life. He came here to make a new life for us and I was to join him when the time was right, but the time will never be right now.'

She sniffled and looked through the window. Martin thought quickly, seeking something to say that was more consoling than what he'd managed so far.

'Perhaps if you saw him buried, that'd help you?'

'There's not enough time. The stage will leave soon.'

He joined her at the window.

'Except there are other ways to reach Eureka Forks. The train leaves tomorrow morning and I'm sure I could arrange to get your husband buried before then.'

'I guess the train should be safe.' She gnawed at her bottom lip then nodded. 'And you're right. A wife should stay for her husband's funeral. Could you deal with everything?'

'Sure,' he said and smiled after being given a useful task. He hurried to the door, but she stopped him with a cough.

'But make sure the arrangements are private.' She gave him a worried look. 'I don't want whoever killed him to know what I'm doing.'

'If ever a man didn't deserve summary justice, it was Eddie Crabbe,' Braxton said when he joined Marshal McSween in the Sagebrush saloon.

'I know, but it's good to hear it from someone else,' McSween said.

For his first task McSween had told Braxton to ask around about Eddie. So Braxton had done his duty while taking the opportunity to probe about his father's demise.

He had yet to talk to anyone who had lived here seven years ago, although he'd been given the names of two people who had worked on the railroad. Other than that, he had learnt nothing that added to his knowledge of what had happened.

As for Eddie, he hadn't had any enemies. Everyone Braxton had talked to said the same thing.

Eddie had dealt with trouble quickly and fairly.

He'd judged situations well, and if a few warning words would work better than a spell in the jailhouse, he'd delivered those instead. He had been jovial, respectful and kind, and everyone agreed that when McSween had appointed a deputy Eddie Crabbe had been the best choice he could have made.

'I'm sure he wasn't killed for doing something wrong.' Braxton sat at the corner table and considered McSween. 'So perhaps it was for doing something right.'

'Eddie often said that sort of thing and he was always right. What's on your mind?'

Braxton glanced around the saloon to check nobody could hear him. It was mid-afternoon and the saloon room was quiet, with just a poker game in progress by the window.

'As he was investigating the first lynching, perhaps he was killed because he'd worked out who did it?'

McSween smiled and poured Braxton a whiskey.

'I like the way you think.'

Braxton was sure he'd only reached the conclusion McSween had wanted him to reach, but the marshal's support was welcome.

'I also wonder if his death could be connected to what happened here seven years ago?'

A loud oath sounded and chairs were scraped back, making McSween glance at the poker game, which had just reached an acrimonious showdown. When the players who had thrown in their hands urged the others to calm down, he snorted a rueful laugh and waggled a warning finger at Braxton.

'Eddie also made connections that weren't there, so don't seek out conspiracies. Everyone says Sherwood Drake and his gang got what they . . .' McSween trailed off and his eyes narrowed as the obvious point hit him for the first time.

'You were about to say they got what they deserved, except nobody deserves that and, yes, Sherwood Drake was my father.'

McSween coughed. When he spoke again his tone was low as he struggled to control his embarrassment.

'We had no law back then. People had to sort out their own problems. When I said they deserved that end, it's only because there was no other option. We have other options now.'

'I know.' Braxton smiled. 'And don't feel bad. My father was nothing like Eddie, but I'd still like to find out who killed him.'

'I doubt you'll get an answer. Nobody has ever revealed who was in the lynch mob. With so much time having passed, I'm sure the incidents are unconnected.'

'You're probably right.' Braxton waited until McSween nodded before he continued: 'So who was the first man to get lynched? Because nobody has talked about him.'

'That's because nobody mourns Leon Williamson's passing. Last month, when I took on Eddie, to everyone's surprise he and Leon renewed their friendship. Leon once worked for the railroad, but he'd changed and every crime in town led back to him. Eddie tried to help him.'

'So Eddie had worked on the railroad too?'

McSween nodded. 'Given time Eddie might have changed him for the better, but Leon pursued the Norton brothers' only sister. They warned him off, but he and Natalie still sneaked away for a picnic. Nobody knows what happened next, but Leon went missing and the next day her body washed up downriver.'

'Any proof he killed her?'

McSween shook his head. 'When I found Leon, he claimed it'd been an accident and Natalie had slipped and drowned. He ran because he reckoned nobody would believe him. He was right. As I couldn't prove nothing, I released him and the next morning he was swinging from the same tree where Eddie was hanged. . . .'

McSween frowned and sipped his whiskey, presumably acknowledging this tree was also the one where Sherwood Drake had met his end.

'So top of the list of suspects is the Norton brothers.' Braxton put down his glass and stood up, making the marshal raise a hand.

'They've been here longer than anyone and they don't like nobody questioning them, so wait until morning.' McSween winked. 'I don't want to lose two deputies in as many days.'

Braxton nodded, but before he could congratulate himself on getting the names of people who had been living here seven years ago, the poker argument became rowdier. Then chairs were knocked aside and oaths were traded.

Both McSween and Braxton rose to their feet. Then they headed across the saloon room.

The players had spread out. Doctor Jeffries was the only man whom Braxton recognized. McSween explained that one of the men was hotel owner Jeremiah Fox and the arguing players were local businessmen, Renton Hyde and Warren Yule.

This revelation made Braxton pause. He had been given the names of Jeremiah and Renton as those of the men who had worked on the railroad.

Renton had his back to them. He was gesticulating angrily while Warren spread his arms, indicating that he didn't want an argument. Jeremiah moved in and grabbed Renton from behind, but he couldn't placate Renton who shook him off and stormed around the table, the other players scattering in his wake.

Warren backed away, although when he saw the lawmen advancing he looked at McSween with a resigned expression. The distraction stopped Warren from noticing where he was walking and he stumbled over a chair.

In trying to right himself he went reeling towards Renton, who reacted by swinging a bunched fist that crunched into Warren's jaw knocking him towards the window.

At the last moment Warren saw where he was

heading. He thrust out a hand, seeking to save himself, but the hand hit the window, breaking it. In a shower of glass he tumbled through the window to land out of view outside.

'This ends now, Renton,' McSween said.

Renton swung round to face McSween, anger still contorting his features.

'He deserved that,' he said. He barged past the customers standing between him and the door and stormed outside.

McSween and Braxton hurried after him, but when they slipped through the door they found that Renton hadn't continued the fight and was making for his horse.

McSween slapped Braxton's shoulder.

'You see to Warren. I'll talk with Renton and find out what this is about.'

Braxton nodded and moved on to Warren, who was lying hunched up where he'd fallen, with broken glass spread around him.

'Renton's leaving,' Braxton said, kneeling beside him. 'This is over.'

He put a hand on Warren's shoulder and turned him on to his back, but then he recoiled when he saw that Warren had fallen awkwardly and his neck was bent at an unnatural angle. Worse, he wasn't breathing.

As carefully as he could, he laid Warren down on his back, but that only confirmed that his head was lying at an angle it should never adopt. Braxton rocked back on his heels and looked to the door, through which, he was thankful to see, Doctor Jeffries was emerging.

'I hope this doesn't become a habit,' Jeffries said as he knelt beside him.

Braxton grunted that he agreed and moved back to give the doctor room to work, although Jeffries' sombre expression told him his efforts would be futile. Two minutes later McSween joined them, having failed to stop Renton from fleeing.

'This looks bad,' McSween said.

Braxton nodded and drew McSween aside.

'We must hope that Renton will return of his own accord, or he might help us work out what's happening in the worst possible way.'

'What do you mean?'

'Warren's fall was an accident, but Renton did hit him, so if people have decided to deliver summary justice again, they could go after him next.'

CHAPTER 3

'Take me away,' Honoria said. 'I've done what I came to do.'

Martin led Honoria away from the grave. She was still as stony-faced as she had been when she left the hotel.

They left behind a plot with a flower placed upon it, which she had picked on the way, and a cross bearing only the name of the man who was buried there.

These arrangements were made at her bidding. With the undertaker's help, and paying twice the usual rate, Martin had got Eddie buried at sundown, thus ensuring secrecy.

The coffin had been taken out of the back of the undertaker's premises and placed on a wagon with three other coffins, giving the impression it was empty. Then a grave that had been dug earlier had been commandeered.

Before Martin had escorted her out of the hotel

she had changed into normal attire, and they had walked along with her holding his arm. Aside from her tear-streaked cheeks and sombre expression, they had presented the normal appearance of a couple taking a stroll.

On the way back she gripped his arm more tightly and they took a path around town so that they would arrive alongside the Sagebrush Hotel. When they were amongst people she speeded up and Martin looked keenly at every person they passed as he weighed up whether they might cause trouble, but nobody paid them any attention.

Nobody was in the hotel downstairs, so Honoria tore herself free of his arm and hurried upstairs. He had yet to reach the bottom of the stairs when she disappeared from view, but he followed at a more sedate pace.

Her door was open and, as he'd expected, she was lying face down on the bed bawling with uncontrollable tears as she released the pent-up tension of the last few hours. Martin quietly closed the door and sat on a chair beside it.

After a few minutes her sobbing petered out and with a sigh she shuffled round on the bed to face him. Her tear-dampened hair was loose and plastered across her face; she brushed it aside before giving a wan smile.

'Can I do anything more for you tonight?' Martin asked.

'You've been kind,' she said, her voice faltering.

'You're a good man, like my father was and like Eddie was. And I agree now that staying to see Eddie buried was the right thing to do.'

'I'm sure that one day it will give you comfort.'

'And now I'm back here and safe, tell Eddie's friends where I buried him.'

'I'll do that, and I'll return first thing tomorrow to escort you to the station.'

Martin got up to leave, but she raised a hand.

'I don't want to be alone tonight,' she said.

Martin gulped. 'What do you mean?'

'If you don't mind, I'd like you to sleep in here, on the floor, or in the chair by the door if you prefer.' She shrugged. 'I'd feel safer.'

'I can do that.'

'And can you organize a hot bath for me and stand guard?' She stretched. 'I'd feel safer.'

'I can do that.'

She rubbed her arms and neck, as if imagining immersing herself in hot water, and murmured in delight:

'You can use my water. I'll try not to let it get cold.'

'Cold water will be fine,' Martin said.

'I'll look for Renton Hyde today,' Marshal McSween said when Braxton arrived at the law office in the morning.

'Which means I'll visit the Norton brothers?' Braxton asked.

'Sure.' McSween slapped him on the back as they

went out through the door. 'You're full of good ideas. So I hope the brothers don't knock them out of you.'

With that, they split up, McSween heading out of town to stake out Renton's house while Braxton made off in the opposite direction. As this took him by the cemetery, he visited Eddie's grave.

When he drew up beside the picket fence four men and a woman were already there. When one of the men noticed Braxton he came across to the gate and blocked his path.

'Wait there,' he ordered.

'Sure.' Braxton looked past the man at the rest of the group. 'How do you know Eddie?'

The man stood tall, his resolute gaze staring straight through Braxton.

'Why do you need to know?'

Braxton was trying to work out how to respond to this chilly rebuff when the rest of the group split up. This movement got the man's attention and he moved closer towards Braxton.

As Braxton wasn't blocking the mourners' way he stood his ground. The man snarled and lashed out, slapping Braxton's right shoulder and sending him spinning into the fence.

Braxton shook himself and turned, but he was looking at the back of his assailant, who was now leaving with the rest of the mourners. Braxton took deep breaths as he fought back the urge to chase after them and demand an explanation for their behaviour.

When he saw that the men had formed a protective huddle around the woman and were heading towards the station, he decided against it. Instead he turned away to pay his own respects.

At the graveside, as he thought of the promises he'd made to uncover the truth, he recalled finding Eddie's body. This put him in the right frame of mind to visit the Norton brothers.

He had to ride past the hanging tree, which made him even more pensive as he rode through the busy depot. A dozen men milled around the warehouses and they hailed him with good cheer, a greeting that was friendlier than the one he was about to receive at the brothers' house, which was seemingly deserted.

A fence, which had mainly fallen down, surrounded what had once been a stone-built mission. Apparently the monks had abandoned the building ten years ago and the brothers had taken it over.

Despite the broken windows, the main building was impressive, but the other timber buildings were as mouldering as the fence was and the porch that fronted the mission looking ready to collapse.

Although the porch roof had so many missing slats it afforded little protection from the sun. When Braxton got closer he saw a solitary man. He was sitting by the door on a barrel, leaning back against the wall with his battered hat drawn down low.

When Braxton dismounted and walked towards him the man didn't register his presence until Braxton had raised a foot on to the crumbling porch.

'Who are you?' the man asked in a bored tone.

'Deputy Braxton Drake.'

The answer made the man tip back his hat to examine him, revealing a grimy face and bloodshot eyes.

'I'm Nathaniel Norton.' He scratched his unkempt beard. 'We'll see if you last for any longer than the previous deputy did.'

'I never met Eddie, but I've heard he was a good man.'

'So they say.'

'So *everyone* I've met says.'

Nathaniel moved off the barrel and came closer to inspect him. His gaze registered disdain before he looked over Braxton's shoulder alerting Braxton, a few moments before he heard footfalls, that others were approaching.

He turned with a smile on his lips, to find that Nathaniel's three brothers were standing around him; they were as sour-looking, rank-smelling and roughly clad as Nathaniel was.

'That's Nathan, and Nate,' Nathaniel said.

Braxton laughed. 'I assume the third one's Nat.'

'Sure,' Nathaniel said levelly.

Nathan had a nearly empty whiskey bottle dangling from his right hand; Nate had jabbed a rifle down into the ground and was using it to prop himself up. Nat was swaying, suggesting that even though it was mid-morning he was already the worse for liquor.

'So you didn't like Eddie?' Braxton asked when he turned back to Nathaniel.

Nathaniel narrowed his eyes and advanced a long pace towards him.

'I've got no view on Deputy Eddie Crabbe other than me and my brothers got mighty tired of him coming around here asking about Leon Williamson.'

Braxton heard the other brothers shuffling closer from behind.

'As Eddie's not around no more to ask those questions, I'll ask you what you know about Leon.' Braxton flashed a smile. 'I've heard some of the tale and I'm sorry for what happened to your sister.'

Nathaniel had been glowering, seemingly preparing to rebuff him, but the last comment made him lower his head.

'Leon killed her and that's a fact, so don't go sniffing around there.'

Braxton figured he shouldn't make Eddie's apparent mistake of repeatedly harassing these men, but that meant he needed to learn everything he could now.

'From what I've heard, Leon was a no-good varmint and he probably deserved what happened to him.'

Nathaniel squinted at him, giving Braxton the impression that he was wondering whether he should confide in someone he didn't know. Then the other brothers closed in on him from behind and Nathaniel waved a dismissive hand.

'Get off our land,' he muttered.

Braxton stayed still for long enough to ensure that Nathaniel knew the matter wasn't over; then he turned, to find that the brothers had tightened the arc around him.

'Move aside,' Braxton said.

'We move aside for no man,' Nate said, his voice slurred. 'Except if he pays us.'

This made Nathaniel laugh, while the other brothers good-naturedly slapped each other on the back. So as they were no longer paying him any attention Braxton slipped between them. He'd taken two steps when Nate grabbed his shoulder.

Braxton shrugged the hand off and swung round to face his assailant, but Nate was so inebriated he struggled to stay upright. With a contemptuous sneer Braxton pushed him away, making him fall over.

Nat stepped forward uncertainly with a fist raised. Braxton thumped him in the stomach, bending him double. Then he turned him round and shoved him towards Nathaniel, who stepped aside to avoid him.

Braxton squared up to Nathan, but this brother was seeking courage in liquor and was upending his whiskey bottle. When he saw Braxton advancing on him he swallowed quickly.

Nathan tried to confront him, but he must have been having trouble seeing clearly as, spilling whiskey down his soiled vest, he swung a fist at an imaginary person two feet to Braxton's right. The effort upended him and he slipped over to land on his rump.

Braxton stood in the middle of the three fallen brothers and regarded Nathaniel, shaking his head.

'The Norton brothers,' he said with contempt. 'I'd heard you were important in town.'

'Compared to a deputy marshal we are,' Nathaniel said. 'We're rich men.'

Braxton flinched as the thought hit him that the only way men like these could get rich was from an undeserved windfall, such as finding the missing payroll. With that unsettling thought, as Nathan and Nate remained on the ground while Nathaniel helped Nat to his feet, Braxton moved backwards, unwilling to extend his brawl with these men.

'How can you no-account drunks be rich?'

'Because the railroad built the depot on our land.' Nathaniel's declaration made the other brothers laugh. 'And now someone wants to buy our mission, so we'll get paid to do nothing again!'

'Then you've found your ideal activity.' Braxton tipped his hat with a promise that he'd return. 'But sadly for you, I get paid to get results.'

CHAPTER 4

'We've left town,' Martin said after the train had trundled along for an hour. 'You should feel safe now.'

'I believe my problems are just beginning,' Honoria said. 'I should never have delayed leaving.'

She cast him an aggrieved look that told him who she blamed for the delay, although Martin couldn't work out why she was concerned.

After passing an uncomfortable night on the floor, he'd spent an equally discomforting morning looking out of the window. She had insisted on their waiting until the train was visible in the distance before making a quick departure from the hotel and hurrying across town.

Even then they'd lurked in the shadows beside the station house before making a speedy trip across the platform to a relatively unoccupied car, where she'd picked a seat at the back as if preparing for a quick exit.

'If I knew what was worrying you, I could help,' suggested Martin.

'I would have thought it was obvious,' she replied in an irritated tone. 'I fear for my life.'

'Eddie was killed by a lynch mob, but they operate in Shady Grove, and I'm sure Patrick Hopeman's enemies wouldn't pursue you.' Martin gestured around the car and tried to cheer her with a light-hearted comment. 'Do you see anyone in here who looks like one of those enemies?'

'No.' She raised an eyebrow. 'He's in the next car.'

Martin winced. He recalled the people he had seen at the station and then shook his head.

'I didn't see anyone acting suspiciously. Are you sure?'

'A man who worked for my father, Finlay Quayle, along with three other men and a woman, rode through town earlier this morning. They boarded the train before us and luckily Finlay didn't see me.'

'Why does all this concern you?'

To Martin's surprise she smiled.

'We've spent practically every moment together since yesterday and only now do you ask me that.'

'I didn't think anyone would really want to harm you, but it sounds as if you have a good reason to be worried.'

She raised herself to check nobody could hear her, but she still shuffled closer and slipped an arm through his so she could speak privately.

'My father suffered terribly during his last years,

racked with doubt and regrets. It was almost a relief when last week death ended his torment.'

'I'm sorry to hear that.'

'While I looked after him Eddie went to Shady Grove. I'd always wanted to tend to the sick and the mission outside town was the perfect place for me to do good. I offered to buy it from the owner Nathaniel Norton, but I might not be able to complete my commitment now.'

'Why?'

'Even though Pa trusted him, Finlay Quayle wasn't a principled man. Until recently I didn't know my father was wealthy, but Finlay knew, and now that Eddie's been hanged, only I stand between him and the money.'

'How did Patrick come by the money?'

She gripped his arm tightly. 'That's not important. My only hope is to reach Eureka Forks and meet my lawyer. Then I can make sure the money helps the sick and needy, or else Finlay will. . . .'

She snuffled and trailed off. This story raised plenty of questions in Martin's mind, but the effort involved in explaining the situation made her cry; he worked his arm around her shoulders.

Presently, she stopped sobbing by which time he'd decided that Finlay could get the money by kidnapping her and forcing her to sign over her inheritance. This thought made him grip her tightly and she nestled down against his chest.

She relaxed before breathing deeply in sleep. As

last night had been largely sleepless for Martin, he relaxed and the gentle rhythm of the train lulled him to sleep too.

He awoke a dreamless time later to find she was no longer pressed up against him, instead she was angled away looking out of the window. She noted he was stirring with a nervous glance that acknowledged she was embarrassed to have slept while leaning against him.

'The first dangerous situation will come when the train pulls into Eureka Forks,' he said, trying to get over his own embarrassment by talking.

'I know,' she said, still looking away from him. 'My only hope is that Finlay doesn't know I'm on the train, but it'll be hard to avoid him.'

'Perhaps we should jump off the train?'

She turned to him and fiddled with a lock of hair as she considered his suggestion.

'No, I need to see my lawyer quickly. We'll arrive too late to see him tonight, but perhaps you might have an idea about how I can meet him without Finlay seeing me.'

She shifted back across the seat and resumed the posture she'd taken before they'd slept.

'I don't know, but I'll come up with something.'

'I know you will.' She sighed with relief. 'I feel safe with you.'

She nestled down against his chest and, despite everything, Martin reckoned that position felt right.

*

'I didn't learn much from the Norton brothers,' Braxton said when he joined Marshal McSween to take over the duty of staking out Renton Hyde's isolated house, five miles out of town. 'All they're doing is being surly and drinking hard liquor.'

'Their father was the sensible one,' McSween said. 'But his sons went downhill when they found that selling up was easier than working.'

Braxton sat down beside McSween. They were on elevated land, which let them look down on Renton's abandoned property.

Apparently Renton had fled with only the clothes he was wearing. He had no money after losing at the poker table, and McSween was convinced he would have to return soon.

'The old man may have been sensible,' observed Braxton, 'but he wasn't imaginative. If he'd had another son he'd probably have called him N.'

'You haven't heard the best part yet. Their mother was Nora Norton and their father was Norton Norton.' McSween waited until Braxton laughed, then he gave him a stern look. 'But no matter how much contempt you have for them, don't make Eddie's mistake of hassling them.'

With that admonition McSween departed, leaving Braxton to settle down to his first stake-out.

As it turned out Braxton found this task to be even more boring than he'd expected. For his first two days of being a lawman he'd been busy dealing with interesting activities, but now he could do nothing other than watch and wait.

McSween had also given him what was likely to be the least eventful watch, but when, after sundown the light-level and the temperature dropped, Braxton figured that these trials would be the norm in his new life.

Before long he struggled to see the house. The night was promising to be cloudy and he doubted he would see Renton if he returned stealthily. Although his orders were to stay back, he figured that, this far from the house, he wasn't being effective.

Under the cover of the gathering darkness he made his way to the house. He stopped beside the corner post of the small corral where he could see the door and the approach.

Before he could pick out the best spot to hide he heard a scraping sound within the house. Then, through the window, he saw someone move.

It was too dark for him discern who was inside, but he wasted no time before he hurried to the door. He listened, hearing that whoever was inside was rummaging.

The muttered curses suggested that in the dark he wasn't finding what he was looking for; it seemed that Renton had sneaked back.

With his gun drawn Braxton shoved the door open and moved inside. The slightly brighter light from outside was shining in through the open doorway illuminated Renton standing with a shocked expression on his face and his arms weighed down with clothes.

'Going somewhere, are we?' Braxton asked.

Renton's eyes darted to either side as he clearly weighed up his chances of running before he settled his gaze on Braxton.

'Not now,' he said with a resigned shrug. Then he threw his belongings at him and ran for the door.

Items of clothing wrapped themselves around Braxton's face and he struggled to cast them aside. He heard Renton rushing past him and he moved to block his path, but half-blinded and in the dark he missed his target and Renton gained the door.

With a snarl Braxton tore a shirt away from his face. He turned, to see Renton's back as he hurried through the doorway.

Braxton aimed at the corner post ahead of Renton. When Renton tried to use it to swing himself round Braxton fired. His shot clipped the post and made Renton skid to a halt. He looked around for the safest direction in which to flee.

'Take one pace in any direction and the next shot downs you,' Braxton said, moving through the doorway.

As before, Renton gave a resigned shrug, but this time Braxton didn't believe he'd surrendered. He advanced on him while gesturing for him to kneel down.

'I didn't mean to hurt Warren,' Renton said, still standing. 'He was my friend and when I saw him lying there I panicked.'

'I can accept that, but a court will only believe you if you stop running.'

Braxton moved another pace closer, but Renton still didn't submit. He stood tensely as he clearly considered running again.

'Whether I'm believed or not, it doesn't count for nothing now.'

'There'll be no more lynchings.' When Renton backed away for a pace, Braxton raised his voice. 'But if you run, I reckon there'll be one more.'

This got Renton's attention and the fight appeared to go out of him as he exhaled loudly.

'You're wrong,' he murmured. 'After me, there'll be two more.'

'Are you saying you know who's behind the lynchings?'

Renton sighed and looked around nervously, as if he feared the perpetrators were near by.

'I'll explain what I suspect, but you'll have to wait until I've got something to eat, along with getting a change of clothing.' Renton raised his hands when Braxton didn't reply. 'I'm tired and hungry and cold and my friend Jeremiah Fox is in danger too, so I won't run. You can trust me.'

'I do.' When Renton nodded, Braxton continued: 'But you won't meet my eye, so I know you've worked out I'm Sherwood Drake's son.'

'I'm sorry for what happened to him. He didn't deserve that. None of them deserved that. The hangrope posse. . . .' Renton trailed off, then he moved back to the house. Inside, he lit a lamp before he set about preparing for his trip to jail.

Bearing in mind Renton's previous escape attempt, Braxton checked that the door was the only exit. Then he guarded it with his gun lowered, but Renton carried out his promised actions with the air of a defeated man.

In fifteen minutes Renton was ready to leave and, after he'd again promised not to do anything stupid, Braxton beckoned him to leave the house first. Renton walked outside dejectedly, Braxton walking behind him.

They had taken two paces outside when Renton flinched. Thinking he'd lied about his intentions, Braxton raised his gun, but he'd yet to aim at Renton's back when a sack slammed down over his head.

As the sack was dragged down past his shoulders men moved in on him from both sides. Several pairs of hands held him firmly while he was disarmed. He could hear other men seizing Renton.

Operating silently, his assailants wrapped rope around his waist securing him and holding the sack in place. Then he was shoved on.

Braxton righted himself and turned to face where he thought the bulk of the men were.

'Who are you and what do you want?' he demanded.

He got a clip on the side of the head that took him by surprise and sent him to his knees. When he repeated his demand, he got an even firmer blow to the back of the neck that forced him down on to his chest.

He didn't ask more questions; instead he listened for clues as to who his captors were, but the men acted without speaking.

This made it clear to Braxton they were carrying out a familiar set of actions; that meant this situation could end in only one way.

Renton must have reached the same conclusion, for scuffling sounded as he tried to break free; he was quickly subdued, although his failed attempt made someone laugh. Through the sack the sound was muffled, but Braxton reckoned earlier he'd heard Nathaniel Norton utter the same type of throaty laugh.

When he was dragged to his feet the acrid stench of liquor invaded his nostrils, reinforcing his belief about who had taken him. He couldn't be sure, but he reckoned five men were in the group, which suggested that they were the four Norton brothers and one other.

Presently a wagon drew up and he and Renton were bundled into the back. They were shoved down between two piles of corn sacks, after which two men sat on the sacks.

The wagon moved off. Braxton tested whether he'd worked out the situation correctly by sitting up and seeking to extract himself from the space between the sacks. He had moved for only a foot when a hand clamped down on his shoulder and shoved him on to his chest.

He tried to move in the opposite direction, but that resulted in a boot being planted on his back. He was pressed down to ensure he couldn't move again. He heard someone shuffling close by as presumably Renton tried to escape, but slaps sounded as his attempt was curtailed with greater zeal.

Then he could do nothing other than wait. After fifteen minutes the wagon drew up. Worryingly this was about the time it would have taken them to reach the hanging tree behind the station.

The moment the foot on his back lifted, Braxton rolled up to a kneeling position and kicked off from the base of the wagon. He ploughed into one of the men sitting on the sacks, toppling him backwards. Taking heart, Braxton moved on.

He gained the top of the sacks, but he was unsure how many there were, and his next step found nothing but air. He toppled forward and tipped over the side of the wagon, performing a somersault before he slammed down on his back.

Groggily he tried to get back on his feet, but his jarred legs wouldn't raise him and he fell down on his back, groaning.

The throaty laugh he'd heard before sounded again as one of the men drew him to his feet. The unmistakable stench of stale whiskey hit him, but worrying about his captors' identities fled from his thoughts when Renton screeched.

Renton managed a plea to be released before his words were cut short, although scuffling footfalls still sounded on the wagon.

'Talk,' a throaty voice of someone on the wagon demanded.

'I don't know what you want,' Renton said.

'You do. Who has it?'

Renton didn't reply immediately. Braxton tried to place the voice. He decided he hadn't heard this person speak before. Worse, he reckoned the speaker had disguised his voice.

'I don't know,' Renton murmured.

His voice was sad; he seemed resigned to his fate. Braxton struggled to tear himself free.

His efforts forced a second man to join the first. This man poked at his face to find his mouth and a tight gag was wrapped around Braxton's head.

The wagon rattled as it was moved forward and a thud sounded, causing the men holding him to tense. For a while all was silent, apart from a steady creaking.

Then Braxton was moved forward to the wagon.

His captors did so carefully, although something that felt like a boot brushed against his shoulder.

Braxton gulped; he couldn't help but think he was too late to save Renton, and perhaps himself. He was proved correct when he was drawn up into the wagon and a noose was pulled down around his neck and tightened.

With only seconds to act before his chance was

gone, Braxton braced his feet and tried to leap aside, but the rope jerked him back making him choke and realize that they'd already secured it.

Unable to move in any direction, he could only stand on what he took to be the end of the wagon and listen to his captors jump down. They stood back, and their silence let him hear again the steady creaking that he took for the sound of Renton's body swaying beneath a branch.

Presently even that noise stopped.

Apart from his pounding heart all was silent until he heard the men mounting up.

The end seeming imminent, he strained his hearing to pick up every sound, anticipating the moment when someone would move the wagon, but he heard men trotting away while the wagon remained where it was.

Someone must have stayed behind to move it, but he heard nothing.

Time passed slowly, measured only by his racing heart as he faced the horrible truth that this was how his father had spent his last moments.

After a hundred rapid heartbeats, he realized that the men had left him tied up in such a position that any movement on his part would make him hang himself.

As it was only a few hours after sundown, the long night stretched ahead.

CHAPTER 5

'That's Finlay Quayle,' Honoria said, pointing at a burly man who was leading three other men and a woman into Eureka Forks.

'Who are the others?' Martin asked, as the group milled in with other passengers leaving the station.

'I've never seen the three men before, but Finlay used to associate with some terrible people. I think the woman is called Alice.'

Honoria had ensured that they disembarked from the train after Finlay and now she dallied, to make certain that he wouldn't see her. While appearing to look around, Martin watched the group.

He judged that they were surrounding Alice to guard her, and she appeared to have some control over them as she pointed at the Hotel Grande, towards which they then headed.

When they'd disappeared inside Honoria relaxed for the first time since the train had stopped in Eureka Forks. Now that she knew where Finlay had gone she chose the Hotel First Star, which was near to her lawyer's office. She hurried on to the door, but before they went in she drew Martin closer.

'We don't attract attention when everyone thinks we're a couple,' she said. 'That makes me feel safer.'

'You mean you want us to stay in the same room again?'

'If you don't mind.' She moved towards the door before Martin could reply, but she stopped and turned back to look at him thoughtfully, while gnawing her bottom lip. 'And perhaps a small lie would help. I'm sure Eddie wouldn't mind.'

She hurried to the door before Martin could make any further reply. With a bemused shrug he followed her inside, where she lost no time in booking a room, giving their names as Mr and Mrs Crabbe.

While telling this lie she didn't look at Martin. Then she left him to carry their bags.

He found her upstairs in their room looking out of the window at the Hotel Grande. She was gulping repeatedly to fight back tears.

'You have nothing to be worried about,' Martin said. 'Finlay went straight to the other hotel and he didn't see you.'

She turned to him with tears brimming in her eyes.

'It's not Finlay who's saddening me. It's what I did downstairs. It feels as if I betrayed Eddie, but I had to do it. You understand that, don't you?'

'Sure,' he said, deciding no other answer was required.

'Then we'll never speak of this again.' She wiped a tear from her cheek. 'It's only for as long as it takes to get away from Finlay.'

'But that might take a while.'

'I know.' She glanced through the window and gave a determined shake of the head. Then she turned to him. 'Somehow we have to resolve this situation quickly.'

'How?'

She flashed a smile. 'I'd hoped you might have thought of something by now.'

When he didn't reply immediately she gulped. He could see she might cry again, so he beckoned her to approach and wrapped an arm around her shoulders. As she had done on the train, she nestled close and that calmed her breathing.

'I don't know what, but I'll do something,' he said.

They must have stood there for ten minutes, during which time Martin's mind remained blank as to how he could comply with her wishes. When she stirred and looked at him, he felt guilty for having failed to come up with an answer; that sense of guilt grew when she stretched up and kissed his cheek.

She didn't move away and when she reached up to swipe a dangling lock of fair hair away from her eyes, he found himself lowering his head. He wrapped his arms tightly around her and their lips met.

The next few minutes passed in a blur until she tore herself away from his arms and hurried to the window.

'I can't,' she said. 'It's too soon. And I can't think while I'm in so much danger.'

He came to stand beside her and placed a protective hand on her shoulder. He looked down into the road.

'I can defend myself when I need to.' He laughed. 'But I'm no gunslinger so I can't go to the hotel and deal with Finlay.'

'I wouldn't have hired you if you were.' She smiled at him. 'We should sit down and think.'

Martin nodded and they sat on opposite sides of the window looking at each other. Several minutes passed in silence during which time Martin hoped she'd suggest something, but she said nothing. As the passing of time began to press heavily upon him, he sighed.

'I can't think of anything,' he said.

'Neither can I. I'm useless at this sort of thing. I used to depend so much on Eddie.'

The mention of Eddie made Martin think of the deputy lawman's role and he wondered how Braxton would approach this problem.

'I suppose that after you've seen your lawyer we shall only have to avoid Finlay.' He brightened. 'And to do that we need to ensure he doesn't see us and follow us back to Shady Grove.'

'That's a good idea,' she said approvingly. She leaned forward. 'How?'

Thinking about Braxton's role as a lawman, and very aware of her looking at him in anticipation, he blurted out the first thing that came into his head.

'We could get Finlay arrested.'

'You're so clever.' She rose from her chair to hug him. 'I have no proof he's done anything wrong, but then, he only has to be locked up until we're far away from Eureka Forks.'

'In that case perhaps I should frame him. I could plant something valuable of yours on him and accuse him of stealing it while we were on the train.'

She nodded. Her expression became serious as she moved back to her chair.

'It wouldn't be believable that Finlay would want a woman's possession so you'll have to plant it on Alice, and it'll have to be small so that you can do it easily.'

She patted her pockets, then raised a finger. She hurried over to her bag, opened it and looked inside. Her brow furrowed.

'Have you got something?' he asked.

She shook her head and snapped the bag shut.

'Everything I have is precious and reminds me of Eddie. I can't use anything in that way. Do you have anything?'

'I have a locket. It was my mother's.'

'That's perfect.' She smiled, but he didn't reply and his face had a dubious expression. 'We'll make sure you get it back,' she assured him.

'I know.' He frowned, then the thought hit him that if he misused his only treasured possession, at least it would save her from having to make a similar sacrifice. 'Leave this to me. You have to know that you can always depend on me.'

'I knew I could depend on you the moment I saw you in the saloon in Shady Grove. You're different, and I like that.'

She took a breath as if to say more, but then she looked away, seemingly embarrassed at almost rekindling their previous intimacy. To spare her feelings Martin backed away, giving her a plain-spoken warning not to open the door to anyone. Then he left the room.

When he reached the boardwalk his enthusiasm waned as he considered the magnitude of the task of getting close to a woman who was with dangerous men in a hotel. He slowed his pace in the hope that a solution would present itself by the time he reached the hotel, but nothing did.

He stood on the boardwalk opposite the hotel, leaning against a wall and watching the windows, hoping for a lucky break. As night fell the windows lit up, but he couldn't see anyone within.

After an hour he became frustrated with himself and after another hour he got cold. He still didn't have a plan, but he figured that failing in his mission was better than spending the rest of the night getting colder, and he moved off.

He was approaching the door of the hotel when he had the lucky break he'd prayed for two hours ago. Finlay led a group out of the hotel, forcing Martin to veer away with his hat lowered, seeming to take great interest in a sign on the hotel wall.

When he glanced to the side Finlay was walking away, apparently not having noticed him. Martin followed the group at a discreet distance. The group moved briskly to the station, walking, as they had done before, surrounding Alice.

Finlay hurried ahead and disappeared from view behind the station house. When the rest had followed him round the corner Martin speeded up.

As the other side of the station house came into view he could see Finlay talking to a railroad worker, who was putting on a peaked cap. Even from his brief glance Martin could see that Finlay was being told that it was late and he should come back in the morning.

Martin carried on for a hundred yards, then slowly made his way back. He saw that Finlay had ignored the railroad worker's complaints. The telegraph operator had opened his small telegraph office, which stood against the station house, and Alice was dictating a message while the men loitered around the door.

Martin reckoned he'd never get a better chance to act. He headed back, planning to take advantage of any opportunity that presented itself. He had covered half the distance when the operator shouted in alarm as Finlay threw him out through the door.

The operator recovered his balance to remonstrate with Finlay, but the group closed ranks, hooting with derision. Their ridicule seemed not to deter him and when Martin drew closer he saw the operator was concerned less for himself than because an altercation had started up in the telegraph office.

In the doorway Alice was struggling with Finlay, while the other men stood between her and the operator. Martin realized with shock that he'd been wrong.

Finlay wasn't guarding Alice; she was his prisoner.

As he broke into a run, his mission forgotten, the operator remonstrated with Finlay, who planted a hand on his chest and contemptuously pushed him away.

The operator continued to argue. When Martin arrived most of the men were surrounding him and trying to haul him away. Since nobody was paying any attention to Martin he had a clear passage to the struggling Finlay and Alice and he lost no time in grabbing Finlay and dragging him away from Alice.

He swung a thudding blow into Finlay's cheek, which made Finlay crash into the wall and then reel out on to the platform. Martin moved on to Alice and met her gaze, his raised eyebrows silently asking her if she was unhurt.

She returned a quick nod along with a worried glance at Finlay. Martin took her arm, meaning to lead her away. They had had no time to move before a gunshot sounded behind them.

Martin swirled round to see that Finlay had fired, making the operator fall to his knees. While the man clutched his bloodied stomach the rest of Finlay's men drew guns and turned to face Martin and Alice.

Martin drew his gun. Then, as he was ten paces from the corner of the station house, he pulled Alice towards the office, the only direction that offered temporary safety. Alice had a different opinion and they strained to move in opposite directions with their arms stretched out.

Finlay fired again. Alice screamed, doubled over and clutched her side. She fell against the wall with a clatter, but now that she was offering no resistance Martin easily dragged her into the office.

He didn't have enough time to check how badly she'd been hurt, and he let her fall to the floor. Then he slammed the door shut and dragged a table across it.

As Alice lay in the shadows Martin knelt behind the table, resting his gun hand against its edge. There he waited for someone to make the mistake of coming too close.

He hoped the gunfire would attract attention and that help would arrive quickly. That possibility didn't seem likely as he heard Finlay's men whooping with delight.

Steady footfalls sounded, which gave the impression that the men were forming a line. Then they fired at the office.

Gunfire blasted through the single window and the wooden walls; bullets pinged and ricocheted off anything metal. At his knees, Alice didn't stir, so Martin returned wild gunfire, splaying shots to either side.

When he'd fired off all his rounds he dropped down to cover Alice with his body while he reloaded. Luckily, the gunmen were firing high and only the occasional shot sliced into the floor.

He risked raising himself again, and launched another burst of retaliatory gunfire. When once more he dropped down to reload, the gunmen outside didn't return fire.

Footfalls sounded outside the door and someone shoved it. The table held, but the holed door didn't: it broke in two, the top half clattering down on to the table.

Lying beneath the table, Martin covered Alice while he reloaded frantically, but when a friendly voice spoke up, he sighed with relief.

'I don't reckon anyone's in there,' someone said. 'So follow those men.'

'Wait!' Martin called. 'There's an injured woman in here.'

He crawled away from the door and dragged the table aside. The office wall was so badly holed the light coming in made the walls look like the night sky. Martin now found, to his relief, that he'd not been hit.

When he was able to see Alice, it wasn't clear how badly she'd been hurt. A patch of blood stained her dress, but she was breathing.

He picked her up. The operator was conscious and was explaining where Finlay had gone; so, as numerous people were arriving to deal with the situation, he set about getting some help for Alice.

He had more success than he'd had in Shady Grove and by the time he was directed into the doctor's surgery she was murmuring in distress.

He placed her on a table. After a brief examination the doctor declared that she had only been grazed by a bullet across her ribs. She had lost consciousness from knocking her head when she'd fallen.

Then, as the operator was brought in, Martin decided he was in the way. He left Alice with the doctor and joined the people milling around outside, where he learnt that Finlay and the gunmen had fled and were now being pursued.

Martin noticed a light in the hotel room he'd shared with Homoria, and saw her peering cautiously at the scene. He decided he could do nothing more here and he returned to the room to report on the situation.

'Finlay won't be troubling you no more,' he said, starting with the most important matter. 'And I'm sure Alice won't either.'

Honoria breathed a sigh of relief. 'Did you speak with her?'

'No.'

Martin went to the window to watch the people dispersing. He tried to piece together the sequence of events. He decided Finlay had forced Alice to send a message, after which he had no further use for her, and so he'd tried to kill her.

He wasn't sure if that opinion would worry Honoria, so he turned, meaning to give her a full account of events, but she was standing up close to him.

Their eyes met, and then their lips met, and then he forgot everything he'd been meaning to tell her.

CHAPTER 6

'I sure am pleased to see you,' Braxton said when Marshal McSween dragged the sack and gag away from his head.

Braxton's delight was short-lived as, when he could see again, he realized that Renton was dead.

Throughout a worrying night the only way to avoid hanging himself had been to stand as calmly as he could with his feet planted wide apart on the wagon, and wait for rescue. That hadn't come until morning, and then, as his legs had cramped up, he had to be helped down from the wagon.

While McSween and Yves Couder, who owned a store in town, cut down the dangling Renton, Braxton staggered back and forth to work off the cramps.

'I'm pleased you didn't suffer the same fate as my last deputy,' McSween said.

'Last night I feared that I wouldn't avoid it. How did you find me?'

McSween nodded at Yves. 'That was down to Yves. His wagon was stolen last night.'

'And it's lucky for you that this morning I went looking for it,' Yves said. He smiled; then, his thoughts turning to practical matters, he peered into the back of the wagon at the sacks of produce, leaving McSween to draw Braxton aside.

'Did you see who did it?' McSween asked.

'No. It was dark even before they put a sack over my head and they worked silently, but one man had a distinctive laugh and he reeked of whiskey.'

McSween shrugged. 'Anyone would need liquor in them to stomach hanging a man.'

'I'm sure they would, but yesterday the Norton brothers were the worse for liquor, and Nathaniel had a similar sounding laugh.'

McSween shook his head. 'I'll need a better reason than whiskey and laughter to bring them in.'

'We might get one. Renton knew who was behind the lynchings. Before he could tell me what he suspected we were attacked, but he reckoned the deaths weren't retaliation for recent crimes. They're connected to what happened here seven years ago. He called the perpetrators the hangrope posse.'

Braxton was only guessing that this was what Renton had tried to tell him, but McSween's eyes opened wide, suggesting that no matter what he'd supposed before, a connection was possible.

'It was rumoured that the men who strung up your father and the others called themselves the hangrope posse.'

'And there's more. Renton reckoned two more men would get lynched and he feared the next one would be Jeremiah Fox.'

McSween winced. 'I heard last night that Jeremiah *has* gone missing.'

'Then we have to find him before the hangrope posse does.' Braxton rubbed his jaw as more details from last night came back to him. 'And they demanded information from Renton. They're looking for something and I'd guess they're still searching for the stolen payroll.'

'You could be right.' McSween pointed at him and lowered his voice. 'But remember this: I know you want to find out who killed your father, but don't jump to conclusions and don't look for connections that aren't there. It's still not certain this has anything to do with the events of seven years ago.'

'Last night those events were the only thing on my mind.' Braxton frowned. 'So I hope we can prove that one way or another, before anyone else has to die in that horrible way.'

In the morning the chatter Martin overheard in the hotel was about the gunmen who had fled last night, although nobody knew who they were or what their business had been.

He didn't hear about Alice's condition, so after breakfast Martin wanted to check on her. However, Honoria distracted him in a pleasant manner and then there wasn't time before she was due to meet her lawyer.

On the way Honoria beamed with delight, appearing the most animated she'd been since she'd given him this assignment. She didn't want him to accompany her into the lawyer's office, so he stood guard at the door and pondered on what his future might bring.

He wouldn't have thought a recently widowed woman would make an ideal partner, but she appeared content about the situation. He decided she might not be thinking straight, that the trauma had made her seek comfort with the first suitable man who was kind to her.

As he was that man, he decided not to question his luck.

An hour passed before she emerged, with her brow furrowed. She didn't explain what had happened with the lawyer and he didn't question her as he accompanied her back to the hotel.

Even when they were up in their room she was quiet. She sat by the window, although unlike the previous times she'd done this, she didn't sit pensively looking outside.

To pass the time she rummaged through documents in her bag, but she didn't appear to find the answers she wanted there, as her expression remained tense.

'Did you have a problem with the lawyer?' he asked. She didn't reply, so he tried a different approach. 'Are we going back to Shady Grove?'

'I don't know,' she said, her tone distracted.

Despite the lack of encouragement, he leaned forward.

'Perhaps if I knew what the problem was, I could help.'

'How do you know there's a problem?'

Martin laughed. 'You're easier to read than those documents obviously were. When you're worried, you move closer to me. When you're happy, you get even closer, and when you're confused, you withdraw.'

She looked him in the eye. 'I haven't secured my inheritance yet. It's been sent elsewhere.'

'Why?' He waited but she didn't reply. 'And where?'

She mustered a wan smile. 'I'll answer your questions later. Then we'll put our heads together again and we'll come up with a plan. For now I want to avoid thinking.'

Martin nodded. He gave her time to put her thoughts in order, but throughout the long and tense afternoon she didn't confide in him, and she accepted his request to go to dinner with a sullen nod. Then she only picked at her food.

When they returned to their room Martin tried again to get her to talk, but she went to bed. Martin took the hint and he tried to comfort her instead of prying.

She lay beside him, not wanting to do anything other than cuddle up tight. When Martin awoke after dozing for a while she'd slipped out of bed to sit by the window.

'You'll get cold,' Martin said lightly.

'I know.' She sighed and considered him. 'I'm sorry. I should never have used you. You're a good man, like your father was.'

Martin gulped. 'How do you know about my father?'

She opened her mouth, then closed it quickly, as if she'd already said too much.

'I . . . I'm cold and I need to sleep.'

She returned to the bed and lay on the edge where her rigid posture told Martin she was awake. He still went to sleep and when he awoke again it was light.

He reached over for her, but she wasn't in the bed. He looked to the window. She wasn't there either. When he sat up, he could see that she wasn't in the room.

Even stranger, when he got out of bed he realized that her belongings had gone. In a thoughtful mood he went downstairs, where the receptionist reported she'd left at first light.

'Did she say when she'd be back?' Martin asked.

The receptionist furrowed his brow. 'I'm not sure she's coming back. She wanted a horse.'

Martin opened and closed his mouth soundlessly as he struggled to find a reply.

'Did you see where she went?' he asked lamely.

The receptionist shrugged. To avoid the embarrassment of standing around looking confused Martin turned to the door, but the receptionist coughed, making him turn back.

'She said you'd settle the bill,' he said.

With a shake of the head Martin controlled his surprise and felt in his pocket. He'd not had to use the money he'd earned from the cattle drive yet, but his rolled-up wad of bills wasn't there.

With his confusion growing he patted his other pockets, confirming the money had gone, although he still had the locket he'd meant to plant on Alice two days ago.

'I don't reckon I can,' he murmured.

Fifteen minutes later he was sitting in the law office. Unlike the hotel staff, Marshal Jameson found his predicament amusing and he frequently caught the eyes of his two deputies, who stood on either side of Martin with eager grins on their faces.

'This happens every week,' Jameson declared. 'A young man rides into town with money in his pocket and all that's on his mind is the three Ws. He wins a few dollars on the first, drinks too much of the second, and then moves on to the third.'

'That doesn't apply to me. Honoria wasn't like that.'

The deputies roared with laughter and Jameson let it run its course before he spoke again.

'They all think that until they wake up with their heads pounding and their money gone.'

Martin considered the three lawmen and although

he was sure Honoria had left abruptly for a good reason, he conceded the marshal's point with a shrug.

'My head's not pounding, but my money's gone.'

The declaration reminded him that he hadn't been truthful. He had divided his wages into two and hidden one half in his boot, but as the hotel had accepted they wouldn't get paid, he reckoned he didn't need to admit that.

When Martin said nothing more, Jameson decided he'd garnered enough fun out of his misery and pointed at the door. Martin left and he waited until he'd covered some distance from the law office before he made sure that he still had money.

As he made his way to the stables from where Honoria had hired a horse he dismissed Marshal Jameson's view, as it seemed unlikely that Honoria would have gone to so much trouble to steal his money. He decided her unsuccessful meeting with her lawyer had made her leave quickly.

At the stables he discovered she'd headed eastward, presumably to Shady Grove. Within twenty minutes of leaving the law office he had a horse, but he didn't follow her immediately; instead, he went to the surgery.

Alice was sitting up on a bed with bandages encasing her ribs and a livid bruise on her temple.

'You saved my life,' she said when Martin explained who he was. 'Thank you.'

Her tone was low and faltering, and in the daylight he noted that she wore black. This made Martin gulp as an inkling of what might have happened hit him.

'Save those thanks until you've answered one question.' He took a deep breath. 'Who are you?'

'I'm Honoria Crabbe,' she said. 'I was Deputy Eddie Crabbe's wife.'

Martin winced and to cover his discomfiture he sat by her bed and buried his head in his hands. He rocked back and forth, feeling tired and dejected.

After a while he realized his behaviour must look odd. He sat up, but he couldn't bring himself to explain his actions while he had yet to work out how the other Honoria fitted into events.

'I'm sorry to tell you this, but I found your husband's body.'

She slapped a hand to her mouth, her eyes wide with shock as she cringed away on the bed.

'And you followed me here. What do you want from me?'

He raised his hands in a placating gesture.

'I didn't follow you. I thought *you* were following *me*.'

'Leave me alone,' she said, gesturing at the door. 'The doctor's outside and I have nothing for you.'

'You have nothing to fear. I don't want your money.' He watched her give a worried nod. 'But I accidentally worked for someone who did.'

He gazed at her benignly until she relaxed. Then

he gave an account of his situation. When he mentioned the woman who had called herself Honoria, she shook her head.

'I thought it was strange when she left abruptly.' She firmed her jaw, her eyes narrowing with anger. 'Your Honoria . . . or as I knew her, Alice O'Shannon, helped me when I was tending to Pa and we became friends. I confided in her, telling her things Eddie and I had agreed to keep secret.'

'About unexpectedly discovering your father was wealthy?'

She nodded. 'And how I intended to use his money to buy the mission in Shady Grove. She was supportive, but when Finlay Quayle claimed the money was rightfully his, she left without saying goodbye and some documents went missing. Before I could worry about that, Finlay took me to Shady Grove where someone had killed Eddie.'

She broke off to snuffle; hearing the sound the doctor looked in on them, but she shooed him away.

'Did Finlay get the money? Because it's no longer in Eureka Forks.'

'The money was never here. It's in a bank in Silver Creek. I told Finlay stories to buy time. I feared that when he found out the money wasn't with the lawyer he'd kill me, but when I told him he threatened me with something worse than death.'

'What was that?' Martin asked with a wince.

'That's none of your concern. I did what he ordered and sent a message for the money to be delivered to Shady Grove on the next train.' She shivered. 'Clearly Finlay planned to kill me whether I did what I was told or not.'

CHAPTER 7

Riders were moving through the darkness.

They weren't close enough yet for Braxton to work out who they were or what they were doing, but they were heading towards the hanging tree behind the station. And they were coming from the side of town where the Norton brothers lived.

That was all the proof Braxton needed to move closer.

The last two days had been frustrating. Despite his hope that he'd prove the Norton brothers were members of the hangrope posse, he'd not made any progress in his investigation.

After McSween had found him he'd been too tired to carry out anything more than a perfunctory search for the missing Jeremiah Fox. In the end McSween had searched alone. Today McSween had again searched alone while he left Braxton to continue the broader investigation, although he'd warned him not to annoy the Norton brothers.

So Braxton had talked with as many people as possible, hoping someone would reveal something or behave guiltily. Nobody had and neither had the brothers ventured into town.

When he and the marshal had met at sundown to compare stories, McSween had failed to find any trace of Jeremiah. They had retired for the night hoping they'd have better luck the next day. But Braxton's mind had been too active for him to relax and, despite McSween's warning, he'd headed out of town.

He'd planned to keep lookout on the Nortons' home, but movement behind the station had curtailed his mission. As Braxton crept through the shadows, doubled over, he became more certain that ahead were the men who had kidnapped him at Renton's house.

Three riders were moving slowly, flanking an open wagon. On a moonless, cloudy night Braxton couldn't tell whether Yves Couder's wagon was being used again, but he could see the form of a man standing hunched over in the back, and the man was struggling to keep his balance.

Braxton reached the endmost tree in the line of five fifty yards ahead of the leading rider, where he crouched down. Working silently the riders directed the wagon past the trees, giving Braxton hope that he'd been mistaken, but thirty yards on the riders stopped; then the wagon swung round to present its side to him.

When the wagon stopped the man on the back lurched forward before he went to his knees, and when he stood up he drew a second man to his feet, revealing that he'd been standing guard over a prisoner. Worse, the prisoner had a sack over his head.

Before the situation could get out of control Braxton drew his gun and stepped forward. He fired into the air.

'That shot was for the clouds,' he shouted. 'The next is for the first man to make a wrong move.'

The hangrope posse reacted calmly. The captor and prisoner froze in the process of clambering off the wagon, while the driver and riders leaned forward to assess him.

This was his first sighting of these men, but they'd all lowered their hats to hide most of their faces. In the poor light he could discern only blank features, suggesting they wore masks. Having only met the Norton brothers once before he couldn't tell if they made up the bulk of this group.

He stopped midway between the tree and the lead rider and gestured with his gun.

'Move real slow,' he said. He gulped to moisten his throat when his voice emerged at a higher pitch than he'd have liked, and his obvious nervousness made two riders glance at each other. 'Firstly, free Jeremiah. Help him down and remove the sack from his head.'

The prisoner straightened up, his animated response confirming that Braxton had identified him correctly. Then he moved towards the back of the wagon, but his captor placed a restraining hand on his shoulder halting him. Braxton waited for the captor to carry out his order, but long moments dragged on with nobody moving.

'I hope you're not going to do anything stupid. Free the prisoner.' Braxton waited, but still nobody moved. He raised his gun and fired into the air. 'I said, free the prisoner!'

The hangrope posse stood impassively, making Braxton unsure of what he should do next, but thankfully Jeremiah broke the impasse when he took his chance for freedom. He shrugged off his captor's hand and moved on.

He'd judged well where the edge of the wagon was, and he vaulted down readily but, with his hands tied behind his back, he fell awkwardly and pitched forward. Jeremiah still scrambled to his feet and with his head down he ran on, picking out Braxton's position accurately.

Braxton figured that if the hangrope posse wouldn't cooperate, arresting them was less important than saving Jeremiah. He backed away, meaning to usher him to safety. His action made the riders tense for a moment, then Braxton sensed movement behind him.

He turned at the hip and saw a man standing up close behind him. He just had time to chide himself for assuming he'd accounted for all the members of the group when the man lashed out.

Gunmetal glinted a moment before a swiping blow to the back of his head made Braxton stumble. He took a faltering step, then dropped to his knees, where he swayed while feeling nauseated and disoriented.

The next he knew he was lying on his chest with his cheek smashed down against grit. He moved on all fours to try to avoid the next blow, but his limbs wouldn't obey him and he flopped down on to his chest.

The ground beneath him felt as if it was swaying, and he tensed until the apparent movement stopped. Cautiously he raised himself again, but he could see nothing close by other than the dim outline of stark vegetation; he sensed that he was alone.

By the time he'd pushed himself to his feet he'd accepted that he'd been knocked unconscious and that time had passed.

When he'd gathered enough strength to move on he could still see very little, suggesting that he'd been taken away from the hanging tree and dumped elsewhere. The sky being cloudy, he couldn't see enough to work out where he was, nor could he navigate his way back to town.

He assumed that by now he would be too late to save Jeremiah, but when a chill wind blasted against his face, making him shiver, he turned his thoughts to his own well-being. He roved around in widening circles until he found wheel tracks; then, with his head down, he followed them.

The brisk walk soon warmed him up while the cool wind sharpened his senses. When he first saw Shady Grove the cloud was breaking up to reveal a lightening sky, so he speeded up.

Sadly he approached the town on the station side. Before he reached it, he could see only too clearly that he'd failed to save Jeremiah.

McSween had found the swaying body. He was in the process of cutting Jeremiah down when Braxton walked into his line of sight.

'You picked a fine time for an early morning stroll,' McSween called to him when he reached the trees.

Braxton didn't reply until he'd assured himself of the dead man's identity.

'It started as a midnight stroll,' Braxton said. He described what he'd seen on the previoust night.

'And you didn't recognize the men?' McSween asked.

'No. The riders kept their distance and they hid their faces. I caught only a fleeting glimpse of the man who knocked me out.' Braxton shrugged. 'He was about your build, but I didn't see his face.'

McSween frowned, leaving Braxton to contemplate the tree, which he was now thinking of cutting down so that they wouldn't have to perform this ritual again.

'It's pity you didn't, and it's a pity nobody heard the gunfire last night. I only heard about this when a worker on his way to the depot found him.'

Braxton walked round the body while wondering what else he could have done to save this man.

'I assume Jeremiah gave you as little trouble as Renton did?'

'Jeremiah was quiet recently, but he had a colourful past.' McSween waited until Braxton raised a querying eyebrow before continuing: 'He spent a year in jail for stealing from Yves's store and before that he was a hired gun for the railroad.'

'So the hangrope posse isn't delivering justice for current crimes. They really are killing men who used to work for the railroad in their search for the missing payroll?'

McSween raised a hand. 'It's possible, but as I told you, don't waste your time on wild theories.'

Braxton didn't reply until they'd loaded Jeremiah's body on to the back of McSween's horse and they were on their way back into town.

'Renton said two more would die. Who could be the last one?'

'I don't know,' McSween said with a weary sigh.

Braxton frowned. 'I know you don't want me to accuse Nathaniel Norton, but aside from the depot, all that's beyond this tree is the brothers' mission, so perhaps Jeremiah was kept prisoner there before they hanged him.'

'If the brothers are guilty, hanging the men close to their own property wouldn't be sensible.'

'Not being sensible is a good description of those men.'

McSween uttered a supportive laugh. 'I agree, but they never worked for the railroad and I know of nobody else in town who worked on it either.'

Even though he was unwilling to abandon his only hunch, Braxton struggled to find any good reason for it to be likely. He shrugged.

'All right, I'll keep an open mind,' he replied.

'I'm pleased to hear it. We need to be sure before we act. Whoever is taking justice into their own hands is ignoring the law, which means we have to follow it or we'll be no better than they are.'

'I know.' Braxton fingered the back of his neck and shivered, reckoning he'd never forget the feel of the noose around it. 'But that's hard to accept after what they did to me.'

'I'm sorry you suffered that, but they didn't kill you.' As they reached the edge of town, McSween glanced at the body and frowned. 'Clearly their twisted justice has a method.'

'Having a method doesn't sound like the Norton brothers.'

McSween drew back on the reins outside the undertaker's workshop.

'I'm pleased to hear you say that. Question everything and don't talk to the brothers again until we have proof.'

Braxton nodded. McSween jumped down from his horse to head into the workshop, leaving Braxton to return to the law office.

On the way the thought uppermost in his mind

was that no matter what McSween said, he couldn't wait for a lucky break. He had to make something happen, but when he dismounted outside the office he flinched.

His brother Martin was walking down the boardwalk towards him. He was escorting a young, black-clad woman, who was having difficulty in walking.

Braxton gave a smile that Martin didn't return, so Braxton hurried ahead and opened the door for the pair. The woman slipped inside without acknowledging him. Braxton looked at Martin quizzically.

'I didn't expect you two would return so quickly,' he said.

'Neither did I.' Martin gestured through the door. 'But what's even stranger, she's not the widow woman I left with!'

CHAPTER 8

'Getting to become the escort of one young, pretty widow woman is lucky,' Braxton said. 'Getting two is just plain greedy.'

Martin looked across the law office at his charge, who was explaining her predicament to Marshal McSween while sitting uncomfortably on the chair the marshal had provided.

'In a way they're the same woman,' Martin said.

Braxton furrowed his brow in an invitation to explain, and now that he'd overcome his reluctance to talk about the embarrassing events, Martin related the reason behind his speedy return to Shady Grove.

'It sounds as if you were fooled by a confidence trickster,' Braxton said when he'd finished.

This conclusion made Honoria look their way.

'So was I,' she said. 'And as I've given all the details of my situation, I'd like to rest now.'

McSween nodded and she got up. She took a moment to get her balance while murmuring in pain, although she tried to mask her distress by kicking the chair back behind McSween's desk.

'In that case I'll escort you to a hotel,' Martin said.

'You've been most kind, but just tell me where it is and I'll find my own way there.'

When she turned to the door Martin gave her a sympathetic look. She didn't complain when he opened the door. He took her arm and carried her bag while not meeting her eye, thereby not giving her the opportunity to refuse his help again.

At the desk of the Sagebrush Hotel the receptionist gave him an odd look when he requested the same room for Honoria as his previous escort had taken. Honoria gave him an even odder look when he took the room next to hers.

'It'll let me deal with any trouble,' he said when he'd taken the keys.

'Now that Marshal McSween understands my predicament, if I need help, I'll seek him out.' She bent for her bag. 'And I can take care of myself.'

She stopped before her hand reached the bag and stood doubled over, taking shallow breaths. Martin gave her enough time to grip the handle before he took hold of it. Then he breezed to the stairs, not giving her the opportunity to complain.

When they reached her room he leaned through the door and dropped the bag on a nearby chair. His exaggerated posture made the point that he hadn't set foot inside and she welcomed the gesture with a nod.

'If you need anything, you know where I am,' he said.

'Why would I seek you out?'

Her blunt question made him open and close his mouth twice before he found a reply.

'Why don't you want my help?'

She slipped into the room and cast a disdainful gaze over it.

'Because your brother's lame-brained attitude showed what you wanted to gain from escorting Alice. I'm not like her and I won't be . . . be bestowing any favours upon you.'

Martin set his hands on his hips, his heart racing in anger despite knowing her chiding was justified.

'I want to help so I can make amends for siding against you. If you don't want that help, that's fine, but don't belittle my good intentions.'

Having stated his case and before she could retort he took himself off to his room where he paced back and forth. When he'd calmed down he accepted that Honoria had been right not to want his help.

She had no reason to trust him and plenty of reasons not to and, unlike Alice, she wasn't pretending to be in mourning. Despite this, by the evening he was still determined to help her whether she wanted his help or not.

He sought out Braxton to hear his opinion.

They enjoyed a couple of drinks in the Sagebrush saloon where Martin told Braxton the full version of his recent misadventure, although he got no sympathy as Braxton's recent experiences had been traumatic rather than embarrassing.

Martin countered with Honoria's plans to buy the mission from Nathaniel Norton along with the information he'd gathered about Finlay Quayle.

'So Patrick and Finlay worked on the railroad too,' Braxton said. 'And Patrick's own daughter didn't know he was wealthy, but Finlay did and he wants the money.'

Martin shrugged. 'Alice wants it too and I'm sure she didn't work on the railroad.'

'Probably not, but she knew about our father.'

Martin blew out his cheeks. 'Are you saying Patrick found the payroll?'

'It's almost certain. So when Honoria feels better I'll question her.' Braxton frowned. 'Thankfully, the hangrope posse is only lynching men who worked on the railroad, so she should be safe. It probably means the last one they'll go after is Finlay.'

'And your only suspects are the Norton brothers?'

Braxton nodded. 'They were living here seven years ago, and they're the most drunken and aggressive men in town. So I have a hunch that Eddie was right and this will lead back to Nathaniel and his brothers.'

'That doesn't sound like much evidence, and you didn't recognize them in the lynch mob.'

'It was dark. Only one man came close and he knocked me out . . .' Braxton flinched and stared into space. 'I'm probably just being paranoid.

Dealing with a lynch mob makes you question everyone. But the man who knocked me out had the same build as Marshal McSween.'

Martin shook his head. 'He's a good lawman.'

'I know, but he's argued against every idea I've had.'

'Your only idea is that Nathaniel did it.' Martin slapped Braxton's back when Braxton frowned. 'I'm sure McSween's not stopping you from catching the hangrope posse. It sounds as if he doesn't accept your hunch, but I've known you for longer than he has and I reckon you should trust your instincts.'

Braxton thanked him for that endorsement. Later, when he left the saloon, he did so with a smile on his face.

In the morning the sound of talking next door woke Martin up. He got up and hurried to Honoria's room, to find that Marshal McSween was there. Honoria shooed Martin away and closed the door.

Martin returned to his room. When he'd bitten back his irritation he came out again, intending to leave the hotel.

Honoria was loitering by her door. She regarded him with a conciliatory expression now that McSween had gone.

'The marshal put my mind at rest,' she declared. 'Perhaps his news might reassure you too. My inheritance will arrive on the train today.'

'I'm pleased,' Martin said. Mindful of his discussion with Braxton, he leaned forward. 'Alice told me some odd things about that money. She said you didn't know your father had it.'

'I didn't.' Honoria lowered her head. 'He only told me towards the end and the revelation shamed him. I fear he didn't obtain the money in a decent and proper manner, which makes me determined to put it to good use. I'll buy the mission and when I'm strong enough, I'll make the place suitable.'

'I hope you get that chance,' Martin said levelly, judging that no matter how Patrick had got his hands on the stolen payroll, Honoria wasn't to blame. 'Others know about the money and they want it for themselves.'

'I know, and to that end Sheriff Trimble from Silver Creek is now aware of my circumstances. He'll accompany the train and ensure no misfortune comes to the money.'

'I'm relieved.'

'So, now that matter is dealt with, thank you for helping me in Eureka Forks and for burying Eddie properly.' She smiled. 'So what will you do now?'

Martin returned the smile. 'I reckon it's time I let someone shoot at me.'

The Norton brothers would soon be up to no good.

Braxton had followed them since they'd arrived in town. He'd spent the last two hours keeping an eye on Shady Grove's four saloons. They had started at the first saloon they'd come to, where they'd had several drinks before they'd moved on to the next saloon to repeat their actions.

They already had been boisterous and well-lubricated with liquor when they'd arrived in town. So when they staggered out of the fourth saloon, Nathan and Nate were almost comatose; they needed to be supported by Nathaniel and Nat, who were also unable to steer a straight course.

They had arrived on an open wagon. It took Nathaniel a while to work out that he had left it outside Yves Couder's store. As they stumbled along, Braxton kept his distance behind them.

He was mindful of McSween's demand that he should avoid the brothers, but he couldn't help but think that Eddie Crabbe had been right: the answers lay with the men who hated Leon Williamson. So he waited for them to do something wrong.

When the brothers reached the wagon Nathaniel and Nat propped the other two up against one side of it. Nathan and Nate couldn't keep their balance, and they slipped down the side to lie on the hard-packed earth. The other brothers laughed and hoisted them into the back of the wagon.

Leaving the two befuddled brothers sprawled on the back with their legs dangling over the side, Nathaniel and Nat headed into the store. Five minutes passed without them emerging, so Braxton moved closer.

He walked by the wagon, noting the snoring coming from the back, then moved on to the side of the store. There he edged forward, until he could see through the window. He struggled to see anything in the shadowy interior so he put a hand to the window to shade his eyes from the glare of the street.

'What's wrong?' a voice demanded behind him, making him start.

By the time he'd stood up straight he'd realized McSween had sneaked up on him, so when he turned he put on a calm expression.

'I'm not sure yet,' he said. 'That's why I'm being secretive.'

'You're being secretive because you've ignored my order to not annoy Nathaniel Norton.'

'I'm following your order by . . .' Braxton trailed off, accepting that his defensive protestations of innocence made him sound guilty. 'The brothers are acting suspiciously. I reckon they mean trouble.'

'The only person acting suspiciously is you. You've followed them, waiting for them to put a foot wrong, except all they've done is to have too many drinks.'

'But I'm not making any headway, so what else can I do?'

'Your duty.'

'Eddie Crabbe did that and he's dead. Renton said one more would die at the end of a hangrope and I want to stop that happening.'

'I applaud your aim.' McSween pointed at the store. 'So how will peering through that window help?'

'Nathaniel and Nat are in there. They could be stealing from Yves, like Jeremiah Fox did.'

'Or they could be buying more liquor.'

McSween looked past Braxton, inviting him to turn round; sure enough, Nathaniel was carrying two bottles outside. The possibility that he'd stolen the liquor disappeared when Yves helped Nat to walk through the door.

When Nathaniel drove the wagon off down the road Yves stood in the doorway and gave Nathaniel a cheery wave. Then he rubbed his hands together and set about loading supplies on to his own wagon.

'You're right,' Braxton said in a chastened tone. 'I'll put Nathaniel from my mind.'

'Be sure that you do. You'll make a fine lawman like Eddie did, but only if you don't jump to conclusions. So today you'll start with the assumption that you're watching the wrong man.'

Braxton nodded and McSween left him. In keeping with his instruction, Braxton didn't watch Nathaniel head out of town. Instead, he watched Yves.

He thought back to the wagon on which he'd nearly met his end. Previously, when recalling details of his attempt to save Jeremiah, he'd concentrated on the men and on trying to convince himself that his assailant hadn't been McSween.

He hadn't thought about the wagon that had transported Jeremiah, but he did now. He reckoned it resembled Yves's wagon.

'My instincts tell me I've been watching the wrong man, after all,' he said to himself.

CHAPTER 9

Early afternoon found Martin loitering outside the law office.

'So do I have to shoot you yet?' Braxton asked when he returned to the office.

'No, but perhaps it's time you let someone else do it,' Martin replied.

Braxton looked at him, puzzled for a moment, until his eyes widened with understanding and he slapped Martin on the back.

'I don't know if McSween still wants two deputies, but if you're looking for work and you want to help me track down the hangrope posse, there might be a better way.' Braxton smiled. 'Yves Couder is always busy. His store delivers goods everywhere and he might want help.'

'Why will working for him help?'

Braxton drew him closer. 'I was nearly lynched on Yves's wagon. Yves claimed it'd been stolen, but the killers have to transport their victims somehow.'

'In other words, you want me to watch him as an unpaid deputy?'

Braxton winked. 'Yeah, but an unpaid deputy doesn't have to take no risks.'

Martin thanked Braxton, but the brothers' plan to observe Yves secretly died quickly as Yves turned down Martin's offer to help him.

'But I'm a good worker,' Martin grumbled.

Yves frowned, seemingly embarrassed about rebuffing him so quickly.

'If I hear of any work I'll let you know. Who should I ask for?'

'Obliged. I'm Martin Drake.' He pointed across the road. 'I'm staying at the Sagebrush Hotel.'

Yves looked at him oddly. 'Are you related to Sherwood Drake?'

'I'm his son.'

Yves winced. 'I'm one of the few who was here back then, and what happened to your father and the rest wasn't right. They sure didn't steal that payroll.'

'I've learned little about the circumstances, so I welcome hearing that.'

'When I have time I'll tell you what I know.' Yves gave him a brief nod. 'And now that I think about it, I guess I spend too much time delivering supplies.'

'You mean you've changed your mind?'

Yves smiled. 'I never knew Sherwood, but for his son, I'll make an exception.'

Martin shook Yves's hand. 'I'm obliged and you can trust me to take good care of your goods.'

'I expect nothing less.' Yves withdrew his hand. 'If anything goes missing, you'll pay for it.'

Braxton was pleased to see Martin return quickly to the law office; he was even more pleased to see he was driving Yves's wagon.

'Yves is selling yet more liquor to Nathaniel,' Martin said, gesturing towards the back of the wagon. 'Even more interestingly, he knows about our father's demise. He's promised to tell me about it provided I don't lose anything.'

Braxton nodded.

'In that case, I'd better go with you.' He joined Martin on the wagon.

'I don't need a guard for twenty bags of corn and a crate of liquor.'

'I'll only go as far as the mission. That way I can observe both Nathaniel's and Yves's businesses.' Braxton winked. 'McSween has banned me from talking to Nathaniel, but he didn't say nothing about riding along with my brother making sure nobody steals anything on his first day in his new job.'

Martin laughed. As they drove out of town carrying his first delivery for the depot, he and Braxton exchanged theories about how Yves might be connected to Nathaniel, and conjecturing how Honoria's money might lead them to the hangrope posse.

When they reached the depot they hadn't come up with any clear plans. This was Braxton's second visit but, unlike the first time, the depot was quiet.

They drove past deserted buildings until Martin pulled up in the centre of the depot. He called out for help, but nobody emerged.

'When do you have to return to town?' Martin asked after they'd waited patiently for ten minutes.

'McSween wants me to meet the train,' Braxton said. 'Sheriff Trimble will be on it guarding Honoria's money.'

Martin nodded. He climbed down to look for help, leaving Braxton to clamber into the back to examine the wagon's load. He found nothing of interest and nothing to confirm that the wagon had been used to transport Jeremiah or anyone else.

Martin was ten paces from the nearest warehouse when a man came running out while slapping his hat on his head in a flustered manner. He identified himself as Cameron Boyd.

'Where's Yves?' he asked, his voice high-pitched with concern despite the mundane business they would conduct.

'I work for him now,' Martin said.

Cameron kicked the ground in irritation, then walked to the back of the wagon to examine the consignment. Martin stood back while he prodded the sacks, but Braxton jumped down to join his brother.

'Something's wrong,' Braxton whispered from the corner of his mouth.

Martin shrugged. 'It's probably always this quiet in

the middle of the day.'

'I've been here before and it was lively.' Braxton nodded at Cameron. 'And he's nervous.'

Martin murmured his agreement and Braxton approached Cameron, who was counting the supplies, his back turned to Braxton.

'I'm confirming everything's here,' Cameron said.

As he wasn't checking the items against a list, Braxton stood in his eyeline.

'What's wrong?' he asked.

'Nothing,' Cameron said, not meeting his eye. He pointed at a warehouse beside the rail tracks. 'Unload everything quickly and leave.'

Cameron walked off towards the nearest warehouse, leaving the two men alone with the wagon and its load. Martin shook his head and clambered back on to the wagon.

He shrugged at Braxton, then drove the wagon to the indicated warehouse, which turned out to be empty.

Braxton kept a casual lookout at the door while Martin unloaded the goods. When Martin had stacked everything beside a wall, Braxton confirmed he'd not seen anyone, so Martin, with Braxton on board, took the wagon back to the place where they'd spoken to Cameron.

Although they had no reason to dally, Braxton directed a worried look at Martin, making Martin stop. They jumped down from the wagon and walked to the warehouse to which Cameron had gone.

They peered around the doorway into the darkened interior. Unlike the other warehouse, this one had rows of stacked crates and sacks, but there was no sign of Cameron. They walked past the rows until they reached another door.

All was quiet. Braxton peered outside. As he faced only the wall of the next warehouse, he turned back to find that Martin was looking at him, his lip curled back with shock.

Before Braxton could ask him what was wrong footfalls sounded. Then a man stepped out of the shadows. He was armed and he'd wrapped a kerchief around his lower face.

'You should have left, like Cameron told you to,' the man said.

When the speaker raised the gun to aim it at his chest, Braxton couldn't disagree.

The man disarmed them. Then they were shoved to the back of the warehouse.

Ten men, including Cameron, were sitting with their hands on their heads in an area where stacked goods surrounded them on three sides.

Another masked man stood guard over the workers. When Martin and Braxton were instructed to sit beside him, Cameron shook his head sadly.

Martin caught Braxton's eye. Although he had seen Finlay Quayle's men only briefly and these two men had covered their faces, his meaningful look said they worked for Finlay. Thankfully, Braxton didn't get the impression that they recognized him.

The next two hours passed slowly. Their guard watched them diligently while the other man loitered at the warehouse door, looking out for anyone else making an unfortunately timed visit to the depot.

The first indication of what their captors planned to do came when Finlay hurried into the warehouse. A whispered conversation with the guard ensued, after which Finlay dragged Martin and Braxton outside. They saw that while they'd been inside wood and straw had been piled up on the wagon. Finlay turned Braxton and Martin towards the tracks.

'The train's due,' Finlay said. 'It doesn't usually stop at the depot. Today it will.'

Finlay chuckled, leaving them to complete the story.

'When the train approaches you want us to drive the wagon on to the tracks,' Braxton said.

'Then set fire to the straw,' Martin added.

They both got heavy slaps on the back.

'I knew you were the right men for the job,' Finlay said. 'Don't disappoint me.'

'We'll disappoint someone though,' Martin grumbled. 'That's not my wagon.'

When his attempt at levity got him a firm kick in the butt, both he and Braxton clambered up on to the seat. Finlay gave Martin a brand and some matches before hurrying away.

They had to wait for only ten minutes before the train appeared, their elevated position letting them see it a mile away. By now Finlay and his men had returned to their hiding-places, making the depot appear as deserted as it had looked earlier.

'Would Finlay notice if we rode away?' Braxton whispered with a sly wink as he took the reins.

Martin mustered a chuckle. 'He would, and it'd be a long journey to town with him on our tails.'

Braxton frowned. 'I guess there's a time to get shot at, and now isn't that time.'

Despite his comment, as he trundled the wagon towards the tracks, he still looked for an alternative. When they reached the tracks, the train had halved the distance to the depot and they'd have to use the time remaining until impact to free the horses.

Accordingly, when Braxton stopped the wagon on the tracks, Martin threw the lighted brand into the straw. When the flames caught hold of the tinder-dry straw, he moved to leap down, but Braxton slapped a hand on his arm, halting him. The brothers looked at each other.

'Our father died because of the money Finlay's trying to steal,' Martin said. 'So I'd like to defy him, but it'd be madness.'

'I know, but then again, we never did have no sense.'

He held Martin's gaze until his brother nodded. Then he cracked the reins and moved the wagon on.

Braxton swung round to examine the depot, noting the numerous warehouses where Finlay's men could be lying in wait. Sure enough gunfire cracked and the seat splintered beside his right hip.

From the corner of his eye he saw that the train was a quarter-mile away, and it wasn't slowing. Then a gunman ran out from a building, coming towards the wagon with his gun raised.

Braxton turned the wagon. His quick reaction saved them from a volley of gunfire that splattered along one side of the wagon.

Both men ducked down on the seat to lie flat. More gunfire rattled adding to the cacophony of noise, with the wagon wheels trundling, the fire crackling, Finlay shouting orders and the rumble of the train.

'The train's not stopping,' Martin shouted. 'Our best hope is to ride on and hope Finlay follows it.'

Braxton nodded and looked over his shoulder. He winced. It'd been only a minute since Martin had lit the straw, but already their quick movement had whipped up the fire.

Through the swirling flames Braxton saw the engine looming up close, it having arrived faster than he'd expected. Worse, his attempt to turn the wagon was moving it back towards the tracks.

The fire and the approaching train spooked the horses into a burst of speed and the wagon shook as the front wheels rolled over the tracks, taking the brothers back towards the bulk of Finlay's men.

Ahead, armed men scurried towards them. Braxton searched for the best direction in which to flee, but the screeching whistle of the train cut through the noise, making him look to one side.

The train towered over them, its chimney belching smoke. Then the back wheels of the wagon rattled over the tracks. Braxton gritted his teeth and hoped they'd escape, but they were too late.

Wood cracked and the wagon bucked, throwing both men forward. Braxton had just enough time to see that the cowcatcher had clipped the wagon before tipping it over, spilling him and Martin over the side.

Braxton hit the ground on his back, sending up a cloud of dust. Unable to control his movement he rolled until he came to a jarring halt on his chest. He tried to rise, but his limbs refused to obey him. He flopped down to lie still. In his disorientated state he felt strangely serene.

Presently Martin crawled along to lie beside him. He shook his arm.

'I'm fine,' Braxton murmured. 'I thought I'd lie here and enjoy the sun.'

'You can't,' Martin said. Despite his closeness, his voice sounded faint, as if he were speaking with a hand over his mouth. He shook Braxton more roughly. 'We've got trouble.'

Braxton forced himself to move. He sat up, swaying as he struggled to focus his vision, but when the scene had stopped its apparent movement, he saw that he faced a deserted depot.

He shook his head and the action sharpened his hearing. Gunfire rattled in the distance while the screech of the train's whistle was also distant.

'The train's moved on and Finlay's chasing after it?' he asked.

'He is,' Martin said. Then he took his shoulder and pointed. 'But that's not the problem.'

Braxton shuffled round and cringed when he saw what had concerned his brother.

The wagon had tipped over and it was lying on its side twenty yards away. The crash had spilt the burning straw up against the side of a warehouse.

Now that building was alight and flames were shooting up into the sky.

CHAPTER 10

'At least we foiled Finlay's raid,' Martin said.

'Yeah,' Braxton said. He considered the burnt out devastation that surrounded them. 'And if we're lucky, nobody will ever find that out.'

Martin gave a rueful laugh. Then he and Braxton joined the rest of the weary men who had tried to quench the fire.

Thankfully, nobody had connected them with the fire, but despite the efforts of the freed depot workers and other men from town, the fire had only relented when it had run out of buildings to burn.

The first warehouse to catch alight was in the centre of the depot and only a dozen feet from the next warehouse. So the flames had skipped from building to building as the fire had taken hold with frightening ease.

All that remained of the extensive compound was an outlying warehouse. Here everyone was resting up. Braxton hadn't seen Finlay since the attempt to fight the flames had been lost, so when Marshal McSween arrived, the brothers joined the lawman.

Finlay's raid had failed, McSween reported. The moment he and his men had surrounded the train, Sheriff Trimble had made his presence known.

When the gunfire had attracted McSween, he joined forces with his fellow lawman to chase Finlay off. As scheduled, the train had stopped in town and Honoria had stored her inheritance in a bank.

'What happened here?' McSween asked when he'd finished updating Braxton on the situation.

'We defied Finlay,' Braxton said, choosing his words carefully. 'Then the fire started.'

Finding that Martin had nothing to add to Braxton's brief summary, McSween called a weary-looking Cameron Boyd over to explain further. Cameron seemed reticent to discuss his role in the attempted raid and he gulped several times before he spoke up.

'Finlay kept the depot workers hostage and he ordered me to keep people away,' Cameron said, his voice hollow.

'It wasn't your fault you failed,' Braxton said.

Cameron sighed. 'It wasn't, but before you came I'd already failed. Three of the Norton brothers arrived earlier and they were taken prisoner too.'

'We didn't see . . .' Braxton trailed off when he noted Cameron's harrowed expression. 'Where are they?'

Cameron pointed at the debris of the warehouse

that the wagon had crashed into. The fire had reduced the building to a smouldering heap.

'They were being kept prisoner in there,' Cameron said in a grave tone, his eyes wide with horror. 'Nobody's seen them since.'

'No matter how I look at this, that wasn't our fault,' Martin said, for not the first time this evening.

While Martin hunched over the bar in the Sagebrush saloon, Braxton held his head in his hands and rocked back and forth.

'And no matter how I look at this, we killed three men,' he said.

Martin turned to Braxton. He didn't speak until Braxton looked at him.

'We thwarted Finlay's raid by moving a fire we didn't set. That fire got loose and destroyed a building in which Finlay was holding three drunken, no-account varmints who could have been members of the hangrope posse that killed our father.'

Braxton gave a long sigh while fingering his empty whiskey glass.

'I know, but that doesn't make it any easier to accept. I was determined to connect the lynchings to our father's death. I got so suspicious of McSween I ignored his orders and followed my instincts. If I hadn't gone with you and if I hadn't tried to stop the raid, those men would still be alive.'

'We suspected Finlay would be the hangrope posse's next target, and he was trying to steal the missing payroll that might provide us with the answers we need, so you did what a good lawman should do. Either way, we don't know what would have happened if you hadn't gone with me.' Martin shrugged. 'The outcome could have been worse.'

'Explain, because I can't see how,' Braxton snapped, his voice rising in irritation.

'Finlay could have killed innocent passengers on the train and got away with the money. Then he . . .' Martin trailed off as he struggled to make this alternative outcome sound comforting.

'In other words, this couldn't be no worse and you're talking nonsense.'

Braxton's raised voice made other customers look at them. The atmosphere in the saloon was already tense, and Martin looked at the door.

'I'm going. Talking isn't helping us.'

'That's the first sensible thing you've said all night.'

Braxton turned back to the bar and tried to attract the bartender's attention.

'You could be right, but this is the second sensible thing I'll say tonight: liquor won't solve nothing, but sleep might.'

Braxton glared at him, seemingly ready to continue arguing, then with a sigh he nodded and pushed himself away from the bar.

'I doubt I'll be able to sleep, but I won't find that out standing here listening to your prattle.'

With that Braxton sloped off to the door and

walked back towards his hotel. He didn't speak again or even look at Martin as he left.

Martin's hotel was in the other direction, and he paused at the door of the saloon to watch his brother trudge away, making sure he didn't veer away into another saloon. Only when he was sure of Braxton's direction did he head off for bed.

When Martin reached his room, Honoria peered out from behind her door. Her concerned expression showed she knew about the day's events.

She slipped out into the corridor and they stood in silence for a while, acknowledging that there was little they could say.

'That was a terrible ending to a terrible situation,' she said.

'At least Finlay didn't steal your money,' Martin observed.

'That would have been a better outcome than three innocent men being burnt to death. I wanted to buy the Norton brothers' mission to do good in Shady Grove, not to destroy them.'

'You're not responsible for what happened, and you can still do good.' He ventured a smile. 'You're a strong woman and I reckon this tragedy will only make you even more determined to achieve your aims.'

'I'm obliged for your confidence in me, but I fear for what others might do. Nathaniel Norton saw me earlier to confirm he'll complete the sale, and he looked determined to exact retribution.'

A pang of guilt prevented Martin from thinking of a suitable reply; he conceded her downbeat assessment of the situation with a frown and returned to his room.

He assumed he'd struggle to sleep, but despite the day's traumatic events, he was so tired he went to sleep quickly.

In the morning when he met Braxton before they reported for work, he could see that his brother hadn't been so lucky in getting rest. Braxton looked haggard, with his eyes hooded and his shoulders stooped.

'Are you any clearer about the situation?' Martin asked.

'I sure am,' Braxton muttered, his voice hoarse. 'I'm a killer.'

Martin sighed. 'Last night you'd decided we were both responsible. Now you reckon you're the one who killed those men.'

'That's because I did.' Braxton gestured angrily. 'I was in charge and you followed my orders. I have to take responsibility because I was supposed to be the responsible one.'

'You remember things differently from the way I do. You took the lead, but I was a willing partner and I was equally determined to defy Finlay.'

Martin placed a placating hand on Braxton's shoulder, which he shrugged off.

'You're not a lawman,' Braxton said simply.

Martin lowered his head. 'So what will you do

today, lawman?'

Braxton scowled. 'I'm going to the depot to complete the investigation. Then I'm joining McSween to go after Finlay.'

'The man behind this deserves whatever's coming to him.'

'He does,' Braxton murmured with a sneer that said he wasn't taking Martin's hint to blame others.

'When you get back, we'll finish what we started. Let's hope that Finlay will provide some answers, but even if he doesn't, we'll track down the hangrope posse and work out who killed our father.'

Martin raised an eyebrow, but Braxton didn't take the opportunity to be positive.

'With my skills as a lawman, you'll have more success on your own.'

'Look after yourself, Braxton,' Martin said. He slapped him on the back and offered a thin smile that his brother didn't return.

Instead, Braxton mumbled under his breath and plodded off to the law office. As he had done the night before, Martin watched him leave. Then, with a heavy heart, he moved on to the store.

He hadn't seen Yves since yesterday, and the moment he went through the door his concern about his brother's melancholy attitude fled from his thoughts as he found himself facing an equally troubling situation.

'I hope you don't expect to get paid for yesterday,' Yves declared with his hands on his hips. 'I gave you a job and a few hours later you repaid me by losing my cargo.'

'Believe me when I say I'd have preferred to complete my deliveries,' Martin said.

'I'm sure you would because, as I promised you yesterday, you'll pay for everything you lost.' Yves glared at him, defying him to protest, but when Martin struggled for words, he continued: 'And that means you'll work for the next month for nothing.'

'But what happened yesterday wasn't my fault.'

Yves conceded his point with a shrug before he went behind the counter. When he spoke again, his tone was no longer accusing.

'It wasn't. Finlay is to blame for the loss of Nathaniel's brothers, the depot, and my wagon.' Yves's voice rose as he catalogued Finlay's crimes, suggesting that the personal loss affected him the most.

'I agree. Nobody else should blame themselves for what happened yesterday.'

Yves gave Martin a knowing look, as if he'd discerned the reason for his comment.

'They shouldn't, and maybe after working for nothing for a month, you'll be in the right frame of mind to make Finlay pay.'

Martin frowned. 'Marshal McSween will start pursuing Finlay later today. What can anyone else do?'

Yves leaned over the counter and lowered his voice.

'Only you can answer that question.'

Yves's challenging gaze turned Martin's thoughts

back to Braxton's reason for asking him to work here.

He wondered how he could make Yves incriminate himself by confirming that he was referring to delivering summary justice. Then he remembered his brother's desolate state, which meant he would probably have to investigate on his own now.

'In that case, how can I help you make him pay?' Martin said.

CHAPTER 11

The sight that awaited Braxton at the depot only darkened his sour mood.

Twenty men were standing before three bodies that had been covered by blankets. Their downcast postures showed that the task of extracting them from the still smoking building had been a harrowing one.

Nathaniel was there and he welcomed McSween with a sombre nod. McSween, before he addressed everyone, drew Braxton aside.

'Can you cope with this?' he asked.

'Sure,' Braxton said gruffly.

'We're facing a tough few days. The hangrope posse is sure to go after Finlay, and if they find him first I'll never restore order in Shady Grove, so I need you to be—'

'I said I'm fine,' Braxton snapped.

McSween cast him a stern look, then slapped him on the shoulder. He faced the assembled men.

'None of us know the full story of what happened here,' he said. 'But I'm sure we all agree that Finlay Quayle was responsible, and I need help in finding him.'

A ragged cheer went up. It gathered momentum until most of the men were waving fists and vying with each other to produce the most outlandish boast about who would catch Finlay first. McSween watched everyone's enthusiastic responses. Only Nathaniel was not joining in.

'We'll do whatever it takes,' Nathaniel said when the noise had died down.

'And it may take a while.' McSween gestured eastward. 'Finlay threw off Sheriff Trimble's pursuit in Walker's Pass. As bringing Finlay to justice isn't Trimble's problem, he's returning to Silver Creek. I won't give in so easily.'

'Nobody here will.' Nathaniel cast his measured gaze around the assembled men, making the point that anyone who turned back would answer to him.

'We'll split into two groups. I'll head to Carpenter's Gulch. Finlay came from there and even if he doesn't return, someone will know where he's holed up. Deputy Drake will lead the second group.'

McSween gestured at Braxton and took a step to the side, as if he expected Braxton to explain what his group would do. Everyone turned to him, but as McSween hadn't given him any orders, Braxton only stepped forward.

'What will the second group do?' Nathaniel asked

when McSween said nothing more and the silence had dragged on for a while.

McSween shot a narrowed-eyed glance at Braxton, making Braxton wince when he recalled that the marshal had spoken to him in the law office before they'd come here. He had probably explained his role then but Braxton had been brooding about recent events and he hadn't listened.

'Deputy Drake will follow Finlay's trail. If that leads nowhere, he'll follow any information he uncovers.' McSween spread his hands. 'Pick which group you want to join.'

The first five men to move joined McSween. Then to Braxton's surprise Nathaniel stood with him. That encouraged other men to join his group.

For the next minute the men made their choice, after which McSween took stock of the situation. He had fifteen men and Braxton had five, but he accepted the uneven numbers without comment.

They stayed at the depot until the undertaker arrived after which Nathaniel said a few words, standing over the bodies. When he'd finished everyone got ready to move out.

Braxton was unsure of the direction Finlay had taken, but fortunately McSween relayed the details of Finlay's hurried departure as told to him by Sheriff Trimble. Unfortunately, McSween's clipped tone suggested he'd already told him these details and could only assume that Braxton hadn't listened.

When he'd mounted up Braxton slapped a fist

against his thigh as he forced himself to break out of the fugue he'd been in since yesterday's tragic events, so that now he could concentrate.

Finlay had tried to steal the missing payroll. Had he succeeded he must have become the hangrope posse's final intended victim. Therefore, finding Finlay could lead Braxton to the lynch mob. So, when they left the depot, he rode at the front of his small posse. He had no trouble picking up Finlay's trail on the other side of town.

Throughout the morning the group rode at a steady mile-eating pace. Braxton called a halt for the first time when they reached Walker's Pass.

Braxton dismounted and gathered his group around him. In an attempt to appear as confident as McSween had been earlier, he tried to give his first motivational speech.

'This is where Sheriff Trimble gave up the chase,' he declared. 'I'm confident we'll do better.'

Braxton looked at each man in turn and although he hadn't expected an animated response, he was surprised that everyone glared at him. Then Nathaniel stepped forward.

'We will, but it's yet to be proved whether you can,' he said.

Braxton spread his hands. 'This is my first big challenge as a deputy lawman, and I'm as determined to succeed as you all are.'

'You faced your first big challenge at the depot and you failed.' Nathaniel glared at Braxton, making him lower his head for a moment. 'Cameron Boyd told me that when you defied Finlay, you didn't try to free my brothers.'

'I didn't know they were there and being held captive.' Braxton took a deep breath and seeking common ground, he edged forward. 'In fact, what were they doing there?'

Nathaniel's eyes flared, this seemingly being the worst thing Braxton could have said.

'The law never trusted us,' he roared, pointing at him. 'Even when my brothers are dead, you still don't!'

Braxton hadn't meant his question to sound accusatory, although when he thought about it, it was odd that the men had gone to the depot and that Finlay had kept them prisoner in a different building.

'My question still stands,' he said, becoming ever more certain that he was right to doubt Nathaniel, even though the other men muttered unhappily.

Nathaniel took another pace to bring himself up close to Braxton. He lunged contemptuously at Braxton, making him sway backwards.

'They went to the depot to tell everyone we'd sold the mission. As we were planning to leave town soon, they were invited to join us that evening for a celebratory drink. That's why we bought the crate of liquor from Yves, but we'll never get to enjoy that celebration now.'

Braxton gulped, now wishing he'd taken a different approach. Clearly Nathaniel wasn't a member of the hangrope posse, and neither had his brothers been.

'I'm sorry,' he said, backing away.

'Sorry isn't good enough when you could have saved my brothers.'

Nathaniel's accusation could have been worse: he had blamed Braxton only for being negligent rather than for causing their deaths, but although it looked as if his dark secret would remain hidden, Braxton couldn't look Nathaniel in the eye. His shoulders slumped and tiredness overcame him as the effects of a sleepless night hit him for the first time.

'I know. I wish I'd known they were there, but all I can do now is to lead this mission and track down Finlay.'

A couple of the group murmured in support of this attitude, but that made Nathaniel snort in anger and advance on Braxton again. Braxton didn't try to defend himself: when Nathaniel pushed him, this time harder than before, he struggled to keep his balance.

He stumbled and had to jerk a leg sideways to stay his unsteadiness, an action that twisted his body away from Nathaniel, who took the opportunity to shove his shoulder, sending Braxton to his knees. Braxton stayed down, catching his breath, then he looked up at Nathaniel, who stood over him with his fists clenched.

'Get up and fight,' Nathaniel demanded.

'I'm not fighting you. I did you enough damage at

the depot.'

'You did, but you're not defending yourself because you've got no fight in you. So why should we follow your orders?'

Braxton got up and backed away for a pace.

'Because McSween told you to.'

In his first show of defiance Braxton put his hands on his hips, but Nathaniel sneered before he did what he'd been building up to. He stepped up to the deputy and slammed a round-armed punch into his cheek that sent him reeling.

This time Braxton got to his feet straight away, but Nathaniel was standing over him and punched his jaw, cracking his head back. Then Nathaniel thumped him in the stomach, bending him double.

Braxton stayed on his feet while staring at the ground, hoping Nathaniel had worked off his anger, but Nathaniel kicked his feet from under him, making him land him on his rump.

Nathaniel walked around him, waiting for him to get back up, so Braxton took his time. After a few moments his failure to fight back made Nathaniel mutter an oath and plant a foot against his shoulder.

He shoved Braxton over. Then, while lying on his side, Braxton watched Nathaniel walk away and gather the rest of the group around him.

The contemptuous way the men looked at him left no doubt that no matter what he did now, he'd lost the right to lead them. Nathaniel sought opinions and when that resulted in a round of pointing and supportive murmuring, he walked back to Braxton, who was still lying where he'd fallen.

'What now?' Braxton murmured.

'We're leaving to get Finlay. You're just leaving.' Nathaniel gestured, indicating a general northward direction. 'Get on your horse and ride. Don't ever come back to Shady Grove or I'll make what the lynch mob nearly did to you seem like a gentle tap in the side.'

To emphasize his point Nathaniel tapped the toe of his boot against Braxton's ribs. When Braxton didn't react, he snorted in derision and turned away.

Braxton did nothing more than watch him mount up, order the men into a defensive formation, and ride off into the pass.

When their hoofbeats had receded into the distance Braxton rolled over on to his front and pressed his forehead to the ground. He lay there for a while, feeling too tired to move and too numb to think about what he should do next.

How much time passed before he heard stones move near by he wasn't sure, but he didn't think it had been long since Nathaniel left. He mustered enough energy to sit up and stare straight ahead until movement glimpsed at the corner of his vision made him stir.

A rider was coming out of the pass. As he supposed that Nathaniel had returned to resume their confrontation, he didn't get up, but after watching the rider for a minute he realized that it was a woman.

He forced himself to stand up. He looked at her with interest, glad of a distraction that stopped him facing up to his difficult decision of whether he should follow Nathaniel, return to town, or slope off elsewhere.

'I need your help,' the woman called as she drew to a halt. She looked nervously over her shoulder.

'I assume you met Nathaniel Norton coming in the opposite direction?'

'I don't know who they were, but I hid until they'd gone past. A woman on her own doesn't want to meet men like them.' She clambered down from her horse and moved closer. She raised an eyebrow in apparent surprise, then a huge smile appeared. 'Am I right in thinking you're the fearless and handsome Deputy Braxton Drake from Shady Grove?'

'I'm Braxton, but I don't know you.'

'I'm Cassandra Stiles.' She held out a hand.

Braxton took her hand, noting for the first time that she was young and pleasant-looking with a cheerful smile.

'So how can I help you?'

While she lingered over releasing his hand, with her other hand she brushed a lock of blond hair from her eyes and breathed a sigh of relief.

'You've already done that,' she said. 'I feel safe now I'm with you.'

CHAPTER 12

Martin had left town with Yves's group only an hour ago, but he was already sure he was riding with the hangrope posse.

Yves was leading four men. Aside from Cameron Boyd, Martin hadn't met these men before.

The fact that they hadn't helped retrieve the bodies from the warehouse told Martin everything he needed to know about their motivation. That didn't change his own opinion that Finlay needed to be dealt with. If the law couldn't catch him, he hoped these men could.

After that, he would ensure that this would be the hangrope posse's last mission.

Yves had a destination in mind. He rode beside the tracks, heading west towards Eureka Forks, which was a different direction from those that Marshal McSween and Braxton had taken.

It wasn't until Yves called a halt at noon beside a

mound that he explained where he thought Finlay had gone.

'Finlay worked for the railroad,' he said. 'So he'll hole up at one of the abandoned station houses along the tracks. The first one is beyond this mound.'

Cameron nodded. While he made plans to find out if they'd located Finlay at the first attempt, Martin joined Yves.

'Why are you so sure about that?' he asked.

'Because over the years I've learnt plenty about Finlay.'

Martin gulped. 'Which means you're the hangrope posse, returning after seven years to deliver justice again in your search for the missing payroll.'

Yves laughed, encouraging the other men to shake their heads.

'We're not the hangrope posse. We're handing out justice to the hangrope posse.'

Martin winced. 'And Finlay is a member of the lynch mob that strung up my father?'

Yves nodded while providing a sorry look.

'And they strung up my brother, Pierre Couder.' Yves took a deep breath. 'Like Sherwood, his only crime was to defy the railroad. They weren't happy with working long hours for low wages, so they fought back against their overseer Patrick Hopeman.'

'From what I can remember of my father, he wasn't happy with working, no matter what he was paid.'

Yves smiled. 'Sometimes men do the right thing for the wrong reason. Back then Sherwood gathered like-minded men about him, including Pierre. They refused to work and when they were run off, they disrupted the track-laying while seeking support for their stance.'

'Only four men were hanged, so they couldn't have got that support.'

Yves nodded. 'Patrick didn't let their campaign gather momentum. He vilified them with tales of their supposed crimes. When he claimed they'd stolen the payroll and nobody would get paid, the workers turned against them. Nobody complained when they were found strung up, and afterwards nobody showed dissent again.'

Martin walked around in a circle, collecting his thoughts.

Although this version of events was different from what he'd heard before, suggesting it was as biased as the alternative version, it gave him comfort. It seemed his father might not have been as lazy and as criminally inclined as he'd thought.

'How did you figure this out?'

'I suspected that Finlay led the hangrope posse and that Leon Williamson helped him, but I had no proof until Leon killed Natalie Norton. My friends decided to teach Leon a lesson, so I joined them. To save his skin, Leon told me the truth. It didn't help him none.'

'So who were the other members of the hangrope posse?'

'Leon claimed Patrick led them, while Finlay was his deputy. Patrick escaped justice by dying, but Leon, Renton Hyde and Jeremiah Fox got what they deserved.'

The fact that Honoria's father hadn't just found the payroll but that he had led the hangrope posse made Martin bow his head. It took him a moment to pick up on the other worrying aspect of this revelation.

'You taught the guilty a lesson, but what about Eddie Crabbe?'

'Hanging Eddie was the hardest task of all, but seven years ago he was a member of the hangrope posse too.'

'But everyone said he was a decent man. His wife thought him . . .' Martin trailed off, the revelations shocking him into silence.

'After the lynching, some of the hangrope posse went bad, like Leon and Finlay; some avoided facing what they'd done like Renton and Jeremiah, and some forged decent lives for themselves like Patrick and Eddie. But that doesn't change what they did.'

Martin glanced at Cameron's group to check that they were no longer paying attention to them.

'It doesn't, but it doesn't sound like your helpers have a grievance against the hangrope posse.'

Yves winced. 'I only want revenge, but when Leon told us your father never stole the missing payroll, they joined me to find it.'

'I assume you've worked out that Honoria

Crabbe's legacy is the missing money?'

Yves nodded. 'It's possible Patrick found the money, or that he stole it in the first place to frame them, but we don't know for sure yet. Finlay will tell us the truth before the end.'

Yves gave Martin a long look, conveying that for him the matter would end there, but that he feared the others would then go after an innocent woman.

Martin put those worrying thoughts from his mind and looked up the mound. He slapped a fist into his other palm.

'So how can I help you get Finlay?' he asked.

Yves indicated he should join Cameron and the others, but, anger making his heart thud, Martin headed for the mound.

Yves urged him to stop, but Martin ignored him. He clambered up the mound until, with grunts of irritation, Yves and the rest followed.

Martin had reached the summit and the terrain beyond was coming into view when he calmed down enough to draw his gun. Then, in a more sensible frame of mind, he lowered his head and moved forward cautiously until he saw the building below.

Four horses were tethered to a fence beside the station house. He crouched down. The other men joined him, and with murmurs of surprise everyone settled down, prone on the ground, to observe the building.

Nobody made a move to capture Finlay and time passed slowly.

'We wait for nightfall,' Yves said after a while. 'It'll be easier then, as usual.'

The men looked at each other doubtfully, making Martin sigh.

'This is the first time you've confronted more than one man and this time your target is armed and is a formidable opponent.'

'Perhaps this is too dangerous,' Cameron said from the end of the line. His comment gathered the most animated response so far. 'Now we know where Finlay is we could leave this to the law.'

'Marshal McSween is miles away, while we're here now,' Yves said, speaking loudly to be heard over the growing discontent. 'Today we end what we started.'

'We never set out to start nothing. We wanted to teach Leon a lesson, but now we're searching for money that went missing seven years ago. I reckon we should walk away,' Cameron insisted.

Yves replied, but support from the others drowned out his comment. While everyone nodded, confirming they'd turn away, Martin was the only one to look at the station house.

What he saw there made him wince.

'Decide what you're doing before Finlay makes that decision pointless,' he said.

For a moment the debate continued. Then everyone swung round to look at the house.

Finlay had emerged. He was hurrying for cover behind the fence while looking up the slope; his three men were disappearing from view as they hurried round the mound.

'It's already too late,' Yves murmured. 'We're surrounded.'

'I don't want to go into town,' Cassandra said, when Braxton first saw Shady Grove. 'I'm still nervous after a horrible experience in Carpenter's Gulch, when Finlay Quayle tried to abduct my friend.'

'You're talking about Honoria Crabbe?' Braxton asked.

'Yes. When Finlay failed, Alice O'Shannon tried to manipulate her. I warned Honoria about her and I'm afraid we argued.' Cassandra gnawed her bottom lip before turning to him with a hopeful look in her eyes. 'Would you go to Shady Grove and explain that I'm sorry, and that if Honoria forgives me, we should meet at her mission?'

Braxton winced. 'I'm a lawman, not a messenger.'

She drew her horse to a halt and nervously fingered a strand of dangling hair.

'Surely you wouldn't leave me to deal with this on my own?'

Braxton swung his horse round to face her. He had meant to rebuff her, but when she gazed at him placidly, he found he just wanted an end to this distraction so he could move on.

'I guess it wouldn't do no harm to speak to Honoria.'

She breathed a sigh of relief. 'Then maybe later,

after I've seen her, I can fix us up something good to eat.'

'I don't intend to come back.'

He wondered what his intentions should be, but Cassandra looked at him with concern. Then she drew her horse closer to stand alongside him.

'What's wrong?' she asked.

'It's a long story and I don't want to trouble you with it.'

'It's no trouble. I don't have much experience talking with men and the ones I've spoken to weren't pleasant company, but I can tell you're different. Come out to see me tonight and I'm sure I can make whatever's troubling you not seem so bad.'

She leaned forward making her hair fall into her eyes; she brushed it aside with an irritated gesture. Then she beseeched him to accept her offer with a wide-eyed look that made Braxton gulp.

'Tonight, then,' he said, making her smile broadly before she hurried her horse on towards the mission.

As he watched her leave he let pleasant thoughts of what the evening might bring take his mind off his problems. Then, as he continued on to town, he took a detour to avoid the depot, so that he could maintain his relaxed frame of mind.

In town, he found Honoria resting in her hotel room. She no longer looked as though she were in pain and she moved with greater ease than when he'd last seen her. She listened to his story with her eyebrows raised in mounting bemusement.

'I remember Cassandra from Carpenter's Gulch,' she said when he'd finished. 'But I wouldn't have thought of her as a friend, nor see why she would come here to see me.'

'She said you argued about Alice O'Shannon.'

'I can't remember us disagreeing. Alice was the sort of woman who can get men to do anything she wants, but women can always see through her sort and I certainly did.'

They regarded each other thoughtfully for a while.

'This matter is no concern of the law, so perhaps you should see Cassandra and work this out between you. She's waiting at your mission.'

'It's not my mission yet and. . . .' Honoria snorted a laugh, which made her wince and clutch her side. She sat down and regarded him while sporting the first smile he'd seen her make. 'Describe Cassandra.'

'It's not polite to stare at a woman and so I couldn't—'

'You looked, and I reckon you found her pretty.'

'She was pleasant-looking.' Braxton shrugged. 'She had fair hair.'

'Cassandra has fair hair, but nobody would describe her as pleasant.'

'Then who is this woman and why did she lie to me about her name?'

They contemplated each other again until with a groan Braxton pieced together the situation. He sat on the chair by the door and held his head in his hands, tiredness replacing his previous good mood.

He felt worse than he had before the woman had found him, because now he had to accept that he was no longer fit to be a lawman. Before the fire at the depot he would have been able to work out who she was, but he could no longer make connections even when they were obvious.

'Alice is not getting her hands on my father's legacy,' Honoria said. 'So I guess I'll have to see her.'

Braxton didn't reply until Honoria reached the door, from where she looked at him with an irritated expression that said she couldn't leave her room until he did.

'I'll come with you,' Braxton said with a sigh as he got up. 'I can make sure Alice doesn't get what she wants. It's on my way.'

'To where?'

Braxton opened the door. 'I don't know yet, but wherever it is, it's not here.'

CHAPTER 13

Two men went down in the initial onslaught.

They had been running down the mound for their horses, but with a hail of rapid gunfire Finlay's gunmen had waylaid them before they'd reached the bottom.

Martin watched the two men roll to the ground. They didn't get up, so he beckoned the rest to stay flat on the ground at the summit.

Aside from Yves and himself, there were two other men: Cameron Boyd and his brother Galloway, which meant they were evenly matched in numbers with Finlay's group.

'We've got no hope,' Yves said, eyeing the two bodies lying at the bottom of the mound.

'We have a high position,' Martin said. 'That gives us an advantage, provided we use it sensibly.'

His positive thinking made Yves nod, but the other two men cringed.

'The best way to use our position is to defend ourselves until Finlay moves on,' Cameron said.

Martin snorted in derision. 'You were brave when you were ambushing defenceless men in the dark, but now you're proving you're just yellow-bellies.'

Any hopes that his chiding would spur them into taking positive action died when Cameron and Galloway merely shrugged. They dropped down to the dirt to use the long grass as cover, their resolute manner suggesting that they wouldn't take the initiative, no matter what Finlay did next.

Martin and Yves glanced at each other and nodded, confirming that they were more positively minded and that they'd take any opportunity that presented itself.

Yves moved into a position where he could watch the length of the fence where Finlay had gone to ground, leaving Martin to hunker down and watch the other side of the mound.

All was quiet on Martin's side and Yves gestured that his view was calm, which meant Finlay wasn't taking advantage of their reticence to flee.

For the next hour the impasse continued, the gunmen not showing themselves.

Martin reckoned this situation couldn't continue indefinitely, and with every passing moment he became more tense. When his right palm became so damp that he had to struggle to hold his gun, he raised himself and, with his eyes wide, he tried to watch every part of the terrain below.

The grass on the mound rustled in the breeze. With his heightened senses he was sure that not all the movement came from the wind; he peered at a position to his right on the edge of the mound.

Sure enough, after peering at this spot for several seconds, he glimpsed someone crawling through the grass. The man was thirty yards away and aiming to reach the summit, close to where Yves was lying.

'They're coming,' Martin whispered while gesturing.

His warning attracted Yves's attention; he nodded, then turned to the indicated direction, but the other two men were lying too far away to hear Martin and they didn't react.

Martin still tried to alert them, but when he edged closer, he saw a second ripple of movement in the grass, closing in on Cameron and Galloway.

He knelt and rooted around for a stone so that he could get their attention silently, but he was already too late. In a rush of movement the man who had been closing on them leapt to his feet and hurried up the last section of the slope.

His decisive action took his quarries by surprise and he covered the last few paces unopposed before spraying a wild slew of gunfire into the grass.

Galloway screeched in pain, staggering to his feet with a hand clutched to his bloodied chest. As he tumbled over to lie still on the ground, Cameron rose to his knees, but a bullet in the stomach made him fold over and a second shot to the head downed him.

While the gunman's attention was still on these men, Martin leapt to his feet. He settled his stance and took careful aim.

He fired. His shot caught the guntoter with a glancing blow to the upper arm. He twitched and came to a sliding halt as he sought out the shooter.

He turned towards Martin. He was still swinging his gun arm round to pick him out when Yves thundered a second shot into his chest. He keeled over.

When the gunman didn't move again, Martin turned quickly, but before he could thank Yves his saviour was already aiming at the second gunman, who followed the first man in making a frantic dash to the top of the mound.

Four rapid shots rang out as Yves and the gunman exchanged fire. As Finlay's man ran along the edge of the summit past Martin, neither man hit his target, but the gunman presented Martin with an easier shot.

Martin repaid Yves for his quick action by slamming a low shot into the man's guts.

With an agonized cry the guntoter folded over. Martin dispatched him with a second shot to the neck that made him flop down on to his side. Then he rolled away down the mound.

Martin turned to Yves, who was raising a hand to him. Martin assumed he was saluting him, but then he noticed Yves's pensive expression.

He froze and listened. Long moments passed during which he heard only the wind rustling the grass, making him think the third gunman had stayed with Finlay at the bottom of the mound.

Using only facial expressions and guarded hand gestures he and Yves agreed to spread out and examine the summit. Yves took the station house side of the mound while Martin explored the other side.

Both men found nothing to concern them on the top of the mound, and they shuffled slowly towards the edges. When Martin could see the full extent of the slope, he stood still and crouched low, waiting to pick up on any movement.

Minutes passed quietly. The thought crept up on Martin that the gunman wasn't on his side of the mound. He turned.

Yves was standing doubled over, peering down his side of the slope. His senses must have been attuned to notice any changes, as he twitched and then shifted round to face Martin.

They both shrugged. They had started to move towards each other when the grass behind Yves parted. Then the third gunman loomed up behind Yves.

Martin fired past his colleague. His shot whistled through the air two yards away from the gunman's right hip, but it made Yves flinch and look around, uncertain where the gunman was.

When the gunman went to one knee, Yves must have heard him move as he threw himself to the right, twisting as he went down.

The gunman followed him with his gun and

blasted off a quick shot that sliced into the grass behind Yves's tumbling form. Martin made the guntoter pay for his mistake when he hammered a shot into his shoulder that cracked his head back before he toppled over backwards.

The guntoter landed on his back and slid down the mound. Yves raised himself to watch his tumbling progress down the slope. By the time Martin had scurried across the summit, the gunman had thudded to a halt beside the man shot earlier, ten yards from the house.

His forces all but wiped out, Finlay showed his hand for the first time. He emerged from hiding and loosed off a couple of wild shots before he scurried for the house. Yves and Martin stilled their fire as they directed triumphant glances at each other.

'Time to finish this,' Yves said simply.

'For our families,' Martin said. He and Yves reloaded.

Spurred on by their success and without further comment, they spread out and moved down the slope towards the house.

Martin took the right-hand side while Yves went to the left. Both men moved quickly, keeping low, and although they were unlikely to approach the house without Finlay seeing them, Martin felt none of the fear-fuelled tension that had consumed him while he'd waited for the gunmen to attack.

In a matter of minutes they had wiped out Finlay's men. Now he felt close to delivering justice to the man who had hanged his father, had tried to kill Honoria, and had caused the deaths of Nathaniel's brothers.

With every stride his anger at Finlay's actions grew, adding strength to his movements. By the time he was halfway down the slope he was running so quickly that a wrong step would make him plunge chin first into the dirt.

Movement below alerted him to the fact that the last gunman was still alive a moment before the man fired up the slope. Martin didn't detect where the bullet landed and he fired off a retaliatory gunshot, but he was running too quickly to aim accurately and he saw dust kick up twenty feet from the shooter.

Despite his poor aim, his gait remained assured, while Yves dug in his heels to slow himself down. Yves skidded along for ten yards before he came to a halt on his back.

The gunman lay prone on the ground and loosed off another wild shot before Yves got him in his sights and dispatched him with a deadly shot in the back.

Yves set off down the slope again, fifteen paces behind Martin. When Martin reached the base he sprinted and made no attempt to stay covered.

As he passed the dead gunman a gunshot tore out. Martin saw a flash of light in the corner of the single window to the right of the door, but he wasn't sure how close Finlay's shot had been.

Finlay followed through with a sustained volley of lead, but Martin continued to run unharmed. He figured his speed was saving him and didn't try to slow himself as he pounded along for the twenty paces to the door.

Finlay paused in his firing, suggesting he was reloading; he didn't fire again until the door was a body's length away. This time when the shot ripped out Martin felt the brim of his hat kick as the slug sliced by his forehead.

Then he reached the relative safety of the door, leaving Finlay out of his sight.

At the last moment he twisted and put a shoulder to the door; it was unlocked and he went barrelling inside. In a few strides he reached the facing wall.

He slammed sideways against the wall, jarring his gun arm. By the time he'd regained his senses he realized the blow had dislodged the gun from his hand. He dropped to one knee and scrabbled around for it as, from the corner of his eye, he saw Finlay taking aim at him.

He had yet to locate his gun when Finlay fired. His shot was wild and it hammered into the wall several inches away from Martin's right leg.

Finlay's poor aim made Martin look up. He saw that he didn't have Finlay's full attention: the man was aiming at him while peering outside at Yves, who was approaching the house even more recklessly.

Having time to act, Martin found his gun lying beside his left boot. With a deft movement he scooped it up and aimed at Finlay.

As Yves was in his line of sight, Martin didn't dare

shoot, which gave Finlay enough time to turn his gun on Yves and fire.

His shot made Yves stumble as he reached the window. Then with a frantic lunge he reached through the window, grabbed Finlay's gun hand and thrust the gun up above their heads.

Quickly Finlay dragged the gun down, letting Martin see that Yves had been shot in the forearm and was bleeding heavily. In his weakened state he couldn't hold Finlay off for long. Martin hurried across the room.

He reached the window as Finlay dragged the gun down level with Yves's chest. Before Finlay could fire at point-blank range, Martin turned his gun round in his hand and swung the butt at the back of Finlay's head.

A moment before the gun hit its intended target, Finlay flinched away and the weapon caught him only a glancing blow. The force was strong enough to swing Finlay round so, using his other hand, Martin followed through with an uppercut to Finlay's chin, which stood him upright.

Finlay shook off the blow and with a grunt of anger he tore his gun hand free from Yves's weak grasp. He faced Martin, swinging his gun down to find a true aim.

While off balance Yves lunged for Finlay's arm. He gathered a fleeting hold of his elbow, which slowed Finlay's attempt to aim at Martin and gave Martin enough time to deliver the blow he'd intended to give earlier.

With all the pent-up rage of the last few hours speeding his arm, Martin swung his gun hand round in an arc that Finlay couldn't avoid. This time the gun connected squarely with the side of Finlay's head; without making a sound Finlay spun round on his heels before dropping to sprawl on the floor.

Martin looked through the window at Yves. Yves gave him a relieved nod, then cradled his wounded arm and slumped down to sit against the wall.

Martin knelt and turned Finlay over on to his back.

'You'll get the same treatment the rest of the hangrope posse got,' Martin said.

With his eyes flickering and possibly unfocused, Finlay stared up at him.

'Who are you?' he murmured groggily.

'I'm Martin Drake, Sherwood's son.'

'Alice's clearly not worried about you returning with me,' Honoria said as they approached the mission.

'She should be,' Braxton muttered when, with one hand raised to shield her eyes from the low sun, Alice waved at them from the porch. 'I intend to run her out of town.'

Despite Alice's duplicity, he wouldn't arrest her, as she hadn't gained anything from impersonating Honoria and now Cassandra. That meant he didn't have to return to town; instead he would stay with Alice to make sure she left.

He figured that in his current depressed state she wouldn't enjoy her time with him; not that she appeared concerned about this possibility as she beckoned them on before heading inside.

With her jaw set firm Honoria dismounted stiffly and moved on quickly to ensure she followed Alice in ahead of Braxton. When Braxton arrived in the doorway Honoria and Alice were facing each other, ten feet apart.

Honoria had set her hands on her hips; Alice was smiling. Her smile grew broader when she saw Braxton and she moved around Honoria to take his arm and draw him inside.

'I'm pleased we're finally all together,' Alice said.

'I only met you a few hours ago,' Braxton said.

'We did, but I feel like I've known you for longer than that, after spending time with your brother, and now that I know about our shared past.'

'What shared past?'

Alice smiled sweetly but made no reply. Honoria, however, found her voice, her irritated tone sharpened by Alice's airy demeanour.

'You betrayed my confidence when I was vulnerable by trying to steal my father's legacy. Then you impersonated me and failed again. Now you're trying another scheme and it's already failed. So just leave and let me get on with my life.'

Alice looked at Braxton as though imploring him to defend her, but as he agreed with Honoria he said nothing. His failure to support her didn't appear to disconcert Alice and she laughed.

'I will leave, but only after we've resolved this matter of your father's legacy.'

'There's nothing to resolve. The money is in a bank and Marshal McSween will bring Finlay to justice for trying to steal it.'

'I know that. The fearless and handsome Deputy Braxton Drake explained everything on the way here.'

Braxton stayed silent. Alice gripped his arm fondly, but he shook his head.

'I didn't,' he said. He cast his mind back, struggling to recall what he and Alice had talked about earlier. 'From what I remember, she already knew what had happened here.'

'It's all right,' Honoria said. 'Alice is skilled at getting information, especially from men.'

'She said I'm skilled,' Alice said with a chuckle. 'Did you hear that, Braxton? May I call you Braxton, because I can't keep referring to you as the fearless and handsome Deputy Braxton Drake, even though—'

'Enough!' Braxton snapped. He drew his arm away, although a moment before he reacted she had worked out what he planned to do and it came free easily. 'You won't make a fool of me like you did with my brother, and you won't treat Honoria without respect at this difficult time for her.'

Alice pouted. When that didn't make Braxton react, she dismissed the matter with a wave of the hand and gestured at the door.

'You're right. You and I should leave now. We have our new life to begin.' Her reply made Braxton blink in surprise, making her giggle before she turned to Honoria. 'Decide how much of your legacy you'd like to keep. Then we can leave you to mourn in peace.'

'You're getting nothing,' Honoria murmured, aghast.

'I thought you should keep the mission,' Alice said, regardless. 'Along with five hundred dollars. I'll take the rest.'

'I'd accepted you were devious, but this performance makes me wonder if you've lost your mind.'

'I haven't.' Alice narrowed her eyes. When she spoke again her tone was low and, for the first time, menacing. 'You'll give me what I want, as you know I can destroy everything you believe in with a single sentence.'

Honoria gulped. 'Finlay threatened me with something like that, but in the last week I've lost my father and my husband, so I'm no longer prepared to give in to threats.'

Honoria looked at Braxton for support. When Braxton moved towards her, Alice grunted with irritation and hurried forward to intercept him.

'Don't think he'll help you. If you don't give me what I want, he'll take it instead.'

This suggestion was so shocking that Braxton didn't resist when she again took his arm.

'Why?' he murmured.

'Because seven years ago four men joined forces to defy the railroad. They failed after they were blamed for stealing money they never even saw. Those men were Sherwood Drake, Pierre Couder, Mitch Douglas, and . . . and Bill O'Shannon.'

When her voice caught on the last name Braxton flinched, making him squeeze her arm so tightly that she winced.

'So that's how we're connected.'

'It is, and the fearless and handsome Deputy Braxton Drake should be able to figure out the rest.' Alice glared at Honoria. 'Then we'll leave.'

CHAPTER 14

To stop him dwelling on the significance of Alice's revelation, Braxton went outside.

A strip of twilight redness was lighting the sky beneath louring clouds that promised rain. Alice would be wise to postpone leaving until tomorrow, no matter what she and Honoria agreed.

Riders were approaching. When they got close enough for him to recognize them he saw that Finlay was riding stiffly, his brother Martin close behind. Some distance behind them Yves was riding hunched over, he was struggling to remain seated.

Braxton drew his gun and moved closer until Martin acknowledged him with a raised hand, showing he was holding Finlay at gunpoint.

'I can take care of Finlay, but Yves needs help,' Martin called.

When Braxton saw that Finlay's hands were bound he called for Honoria. She came out quickly, looking pleased to have been given a task that saved her from having to deal with Alice's demands.

Alice followed her out and leaned against the doorframe with a smile on her face. The smile died when she saw Finlay.

'How did you capture him?' she called to Martin.

'I had plenty of help,' Martin said, eyeing her with shock. 'But Yves and I are the only ones to make it back.'

Martin raised a hand when Braxton and Alice fired questions at him. Braxton helped Honoria direct Yves inside. When he came out, Alice was smiling at the glowering Martin, while Martin had ordered Finlay to sit on the ground with his hands on his head.

Figuring she had a right to hear everything, he and Martin exchanged stories. After the revelations each had heard separately, the full story surprised neither man.

This left them with a decision to make. Neither man met the other's eye, so Braxton gestured for Alice to offer an opinion first.

'Hang him,' she said. 'Finlay deserves the same kind of mercy he gave my father, and your father.'

Braxton looked at Martin, assuming his brother would take the contrary view, but to his surprise Martin nodded.

'Finlay tried to shoot his way out of trouble and he almost succeeded. A man like him deserves to suffer the same punishment he meted out.'

Braxton glanced at the mission. 'And I assume the

fourth person with a stake in Finlay's fate would agree with you?'

'Sure.'

'Then it doesn't matter what I think we should do.'

'It does,' Martin and Alice said together. Martin directed a warm look at Alice for the first time.

Braxton tried to think of an argument against the proposal, but nothing would come. Darkness was closing in and there was the threat of rain in the air; he didn't welcome having a long debate. He looked Finlay in the eye.

Finlay glared back at him with a surly expression.

'You got anything to say?' Braxton asked.

'Patrick Hopeman stole the payroll and framed your father,' Finlay said. 'None of us knew that back then. If anyone should have faced the rope, it was him.'

'I might have believed your protestations of innocence if you hadn't chased after the payroll money.'

'And you tried to kill Honoria and an operator in Eureka Forks,' Martin added.

Braxton waited for Finlay to excuse himself further, but when he only smirked and spat on the ground, he turned away.

'He gets justice tonight,' Braxton said.

Martin frowned, suggesting that he had expected him to talk them out of doing this before he stepped aside, letting Braxton take control of their prisoner. However, Braxton bundled Finlay back on to his horse while Martin collected rope from the mission.

When they moved on towards town, Braxton took up the rear. Alice and Martin rode to either side of Finlay, who rode slowly while looking around. Presumably he was seeking a distraction to help him escape, but with the darkness growing deeper nobody was venturing out of town.

In a final confirmation that he had been involved in what had happened here seven years ago, Finlay didn't need shepherding to their destination. When he stopped before the hanging tree he chuckled.

'Your kin sure did beg for mercy before the end,' he said. 'Even if they didn't take the money, they didn't deserve no mercy and they didn't get none.'

Braxton couldn't see what he hoped to gain by goading them, but Martin cut off his taunts by drawing alongside and cuffing him about the head.

After that Finlay sat quietly in the saddle, his bound hands before him, while Martin looped a coil of rope around his neck.

He then set about securing the rope. Without Yves's experience, he took a while to decide to loop the other end over a stubby branch on the nearest tree, leaving the rope slack but in a position where it could be tightened readily.

The preparations completed, Martin, Braxton and Alice stood before Finlay's horse. Everyone's expression was pensive and Braxton presumed that, like him, they were thinking about the person they'd lost while giving Finlay a chance to say something that would make sense of the situation.

Finlay said nothing. As Finlay's capture had let him regain his desire to be the responsible one, Braxton stepped forward, intending to take control of the formalities.

He had worked out the required actions to tighten the rope and move Finlay's mount, but he found he couldn't take a second pace. For a moment he stood awkwardly; then he turned to the others.

'We can't do this,' he said. 'We're better than Finlay and the others who hanged our kin.'

Up on his horse Finlay snorted with contempt, but Martin and Alice both lowered their heads. With that effective approval of his decision, Braxton walked past Finlay.

He walked slowly to give them a chance to stop him, but neither person moved. Braxton grabbed the end of the rope.

'If you haven't got the guts to do it, I sure as hell have,' a voice said from the shadows.

Nathaniel stepped into view, his gun drawn but held low.

'What are you doing here?' Braxton asked. 'The last I saw of you, you were heading into Walker's Pass.'

'We followed Finlay's trail to a station house. The others are dealing with the bodies while I followed his trail. After I warned you off, I didn't expect to find you at the end of it.'

'Our argument don't matter now. We have Finlay.'

Nathaniel glared at him; it seemed as if he'd continue their disagreement until, with a grunt, he ducked under the rope. He barged Braxton aside and moved on to look up at Finlay.

'You burnt down the depot and killed my brothers,' he said. 'Now you die.'

'Not today,' Martin said with a weary sigh. 'You may have the guts to do this, but nobody will get summary justice in Shady Grove again.'

Nathaniel shrugged. 'Finlay can be the last.'

Martin looked at his brother for support; and Braxton stepped forward.

'Marshal McSween will have picked up the same clues you did,' he said. 'He'll work out where Finlay holed up, so he'll arrive soon. He can decide about Finlay's crimes, not us.'

'There's nothing to decide. My brothers are dead and nothing nobody can say will change that.'

'I know, but Finlay didn't kill them.'

'He raided the depot and burnt it down. They were—'

'He didn't kill them,' Braxton shouted, drowning Nathaniel's words. 'I did!'

To Braxton's surprise, having uttered the dark revelation that had been eating him up inside for the last few days, he felt calm. He met Nathaniel's incredulous gaze with ease.

'You were being held prisoner,' Nathaniel murmured. 'You're a useless lawman, but you're not responsible.'

'Finlay ordered me to place a burning wagon across the tracks.' Braxton raised a hand when Martin started speaking, presumably to share the blame. 'I defied him, but during the chaos of the shooting and the train hurtling along, the wagon upturned and the fire got loose.'

Nathaniel opened and closed his mouth as he struggled to find a reply. He settled for the response Braxton had expected by launching a swinging punch that slammed into the lawman's cheek. Braxton didn't try to defend himself and the blow knocked him aside.

When Braxton had righted himself, Nathaniel leapt at him with his left hand held clawlike, his right hand brandishing his gun like a club. He hit Braxton in the chest, forcing him to take rapid steps backwards until he toppled over on to his back.

With a snarl Nathaniel raised himself to pistol-whip him about the side of the head. This time Braxton thrust up an arm, deflecting the blow and making Nathaniel drop his gun. With Nathaniel off balance Braxton kicked upward, knocking his opponent aside, while in retaliation Nathaniel swiped a punch that whistled by Braxton's nose.

Braxton leapt on him and the two men rolled on to their sides. Then they tussled and scrambled over each other in the dirt while thudding short-armed punches into each other's bodies.

As they were close together, the blows landed without much force, but neither man relented, even when their stuttering progress sent them into the path of Finlay's horse. When the mount kicked up its legs to avoid them, Martin joined in the fray and dragged the men apart.

Even when he'd separated them and they'd gained their feet both men aimed punches at each other. Braxton was determined to continue fighting, but then Alice shouted in alarm, bringing him to his senses.

He stopped trying to land a punch on Nathaniel and turned to find that Finlay had got down off his horse. Even with his hands still bound before him and the rope around his neck, he'd found Nathaniel's dropped gun.

Braxton managed to mutter a warning to Martin before Nathaniel took advantage of the distraction to hammer a round-armed punch into his jaw that sent him reeling. Braxton slammed down on his back where he lay blinking as he shook off the blow.

When he got to his feet, everyone was now aware that while they'd been fighting Finlay had turned the tables on them. They were watching Finlay with horror etched into their features.

'I knew none of you had the guts to do this,' Finlay gloated. 'Your kin barely put up a fight and neither did you.'

Nathaniel roared with anger. 'The only mistake those men made was to be killed by a no-account varmint like you.'

Nathaniel charged at Finlay. He had covered half

the distance before Finlay fired, his shot slicing into Nathaniel's stomach.

Nathaniel ran on for two paces before he stumbled and dropped to his knees. He gazed at Finlay with contempt while swaying. Then he keeled over.

'He died bravely,' Finlay said with a shrug. 'You'll just die.'

CHAPTER 15

Braxton raised his hands while moving away to distract Finlay's attention from the other two.

Finlay followed him with his gun until he jerked to a halt, having moved to the limit of the hangrope's reach. He raised his hands to his throat to free himself and the delay let Alice edge away in the opposite direction for several paces.

Martin had tied the noose tightly and Finlay struggled to prise it away. After a few unsuccessful tugs with his bound hands, he stopped trying and aimed the gun at Braxton who, undeterred, kept moving away.

Martin moved towards Finlay, walking bent forward on his toes as he prepared to make a run for him when it looked as if Finlay was preparing to shoot.

He was ten paces away when Alice ran for her horse. Braxton reckoned she'd have been better served by seeking cover in the gathering darkness and as it turned out her spooked mount skittered away from her.

The movement caught Finlay's attention. His gun aimed at Braxton, he glanced at Alice as he sized up the danger he faced.

He smiled, dismissing her as a threat, and firmed his gun arm. Braxton saw the intent in his eyes and ran towards him, determined that, if nothing else, he would give his brother a chance to survive.

'No!' Martin shouted as he too ran towards Finlay.

Then Finlay fired. Braxton ducked away and to his relief the shot missed him.

Finlay's second wild shot sliced into the ground at Braxton's feet; and when he raised his head he saw Finlay pacing backwards rapidly, a sight that puzzled him until Martin gestured at the tree, alerting him to what had happened.

In seeking to flee from Finlay's gunfire, Alice's spooked horse had tried to run between the trees. In its frantic haste to get away, the rope that was securing Finlay had caught around the horse's legs.

Even as Braxton worked out what had happened, Finlay's feet left the ground and he flew up into the air, coming to a shuddering halt several feet off the ground. The horse then broke free from the rope, but the rope snagged on a branch and Finlay didn't drop down.

Finlay twitched and kicked. While mustering a desperate gurgling oath of defiance, he blasted a wild gunshot that kicked up dust five yards from Braxton, but though he struggled to keep his grip of the gun it dropped to the ground.

'That was an accident,' Alice said, hurrying back, although she averted her eyes from Finlay's desperate situation.

'It wasn't,' Martin said. 'If Finlay hadn't—'

'What happened doesn't matter!' Braxton shouted. 'Free the rope. We still have enough time to save him.'

When Alice didn't move, he hurried towards the tree, but Martin intercepted him.

'There's no hurry,' he said, as he grabbed Braxton's shoulder.

Braxton fought to free himself; then, with a sigh, he relented. The two brothers stood, contemplating the snagged rope.

It had caught on a short branch. Finlay's movements were threatening to tear the rope loose. If Braxton chose, he could, with the flick of the wrist, let Finlay drop to the ground. But he didn't move.

Finlay's reedy gasps for air sounded behind him, mingled with creaking as the branch swayed in the wind.

'Marshal McSween will never believe Finlay hanged himself by accident,' Braxton said.

'Except that's the truth,' Martin said. 'Finlay killed Nathaniel and he aimed to kill us, but his gunfire spooked the horse and it tried to bolt.'

'That was the only way this could end,' Alice said when Braxton frowned. 'Seven years ago Finlay hanged our kin and today he hanged himself.'

Braxton continued to look at the rope. He could shake it loose, but long moments passed in which he didn't move. He accepted that he'd never do it.

Instead, he stood between Martin and Alice. All three looked towards town, with their backs to the hanging tree.

Presently, Finlay fell silent, but the steady creaking continued. Before long the wind dropped, then the creaking stopped too.

'How much longer is he going to be in there?' Martin asked. He was striding back and forth in front of the mission doorway.

'McSween is a dutiful lawman,' Braxton said. 'He'll hear what everyone has to say before he makes his judgment.'

This morning McSween had arrived at the mission, having followed the same clues about Finlay's movements as Nathaniel had. He had listened to Martin's and Braxton's versions of events with his usual taciturn demeanour before going into the mission to hear what Alice had to say, along with Honoria and the recuperating Yves.

'We did nothing wrong,' Martin said. 'He has to believe that.'

'He might, but did we do right?'

Martin said nothing as someone was moving beyond the mission door. It was Alice who emerged. She was sporting a lively smile.

'Don't look so glum,' she declared. 'We did nothing wrong.'

'I keep telling Braxton that,' Martin said.

'It looks like the marshal will conclude that, as he has said I can go.' When both men nodded she set her hands on her hips. 'The only remaining question is, which one of you do I take with me?'

'I'm not going nowhere,' Braxton said with an exasperated expelling of air. Then he smiled: he'd made a declaration that yesterday he hadn't thought he'd make. 'I'm staying in Shady Grove.'

'So if I've achieved nothing else, I've helped you decide that.' Alice looked at Martin. 'Am I forgiven?'

'No!' Then Martin mustered a smile too. 'But I don't bear you a grudge, even if Honoria might.'

'We reached an agreement. It's less than I wanted originally, but last night ended matters in a more agreeable manner than I thought it would.'

'So you didn't tell Honoria the truth about her father and husband?'

'No. She must suspect something as she didn't argue with me, but she doesn't deserve to have her memories tarnished.'

'I'm pleased to hear you can do nice things sometimes.'

'Of course I can, as you should know.' When that made Martin bristle, she leaned forward and brushed a dangling strand of hair from her eyes. 'Are both of you sure you don't want to join me? I'm a wealthy woman now and I might not be safe travelling all alone.'

Martin waved a dismissive hand at her and turned away, leaving Braxton to reply for both of them.

'Someone probably should go with you for protection.' He paused for effect. 'But I reckon the people you meet will have to look out for themselves.'

She laughed and started walking to her horse.

'Perhaps another day,' she said when she'd mounted up. 'I'll miss the fearless and handsome Braxton and the kind and gentle Martin.'

They both nodded, but she took her time leaving, perhaps giving them a chance to reconsider. Neither man did, although they followed her horse for a few paces, then watched her leave.

'Alice didn't tell Honoria what she knows,' Martin said when she was a hundred yards away. 'So I assume we'll keep what we know secret from her too?'

'Sure,' Braxton said. 'If nothing else, some of the payroll ended up with Bill O'Shannon's daughter while Honoria will put the rest to good use.'

Alice was a dot on the horizon when McSween came out of the mission. For long moments he contemplated them. Then he nodded.

'I accept you were both tempted to hang Finlay,' he said. 'But I'm convinced that what happened was an accident.'

Braxton sighed with relief. 'We won't deny that we almost did it, but in the end we couldn't go through with it.'

'I'm pleased to hear that.' McSween rubbed his

jaw. 'Although one thing still troubles me. It takes a while for a man to die on the end of a hangrope, but it seems you just couldn't free the rope in time.'

The brothers both stared straight ahead.

'I regret we failed,' McSween went on, 'but my bigger regret is that I couldn't talk Nathaniel round to letting justice prevail. I owed him an apology.'

'Maybe, but then again, Nathaniel never did have much sense.'

They stood in silence for a while until McSween walked over to his horse. He mounted up, leaving the two men standing thoughtfully outside the mission.

Honoria didn't come out, so the brothers joined him in riding back to town. Nobody spoke again until they approached the hanging tree.

'Your first order will be to get someone to chop down this tree,' McSween said.

'I'll gladly do that myself,' Braxton said. He glanced at Martin who nodded in support.

'And then, since the hangrope posse are all dead, that should put an end to this. The rule of law will prevail from now on.'

'The situation is over as far as we're concerned, and Alice was content. I guess it's up to you whether you charge Yves.'

'In matters of revenge it's hard to prove the facts either way and with the rest of Yves's alleged lynch mob dead, I doubt anything could be achieved by arresting him when he recovers.'

Braxton smiled. 'So that just leaves the family of

the fourth man who was hanged, Mitch Douglas, to be told the truth; not that I've heard anyone mention them.'

McSween jutted his jaw. 'His family are content with how this turned out.'

'You mean you know them?'

McSween turned to Braxton and winked. 'Mitch was my sister's husband.'

McSween stayed until Braxton ruefully rubbed the back of his head. Then he hurried his horse on, leaving the two men standing beside the hanging tree.

'Come on,' Braxton said after a while. 'We have a tree to chop down.'